ALSO BY
RACHEL TOOR

Admissions Confidential: An Insider's
Account of the Elite College Selection Process

The Pig and I

Personal Record: A Love Affair with Running

ON THE
ROAD
TO FIND OUT

ON
RO
TO FIN

THE
AD
D OUT

rachel toor

farrar straus giroux / new york

This is a work of fiction. All of the places, characters, organizations, and events
portrayed in this novel are either products of the author's imagination or
are used fictitiously. Except for the 86-year-old runner at the Red Dress Run.
While that race doesn't exist, there is an 86-year-old runner named Bob Hayes
who lives in Montana and continues to kick butt in marathons and 50Ks and to
inspire the author.

Farrar Straus Giroux Books for Young Readers
175 Fifth Avenue, New York 10010

Printed in the United States of America
Designed by Andrew Arnold
First edition, 2014
1   3   5   7   9   10   8   6   4   2

macteenbooks.com

Library of Congress Cataloging-in-Publication Data
Toor, Rachel.
    On the road to find out / Rachel Toor.
        pages cm
    Summary: Alice Evelyn Davis, seventeen, has generally gotten all she wants
from life but when her college of choice rejects her, problems with her best friend
arise, and she faces an unexpected loss, her newfound interest in running helps
get her through.
    ISBN 978-0-374-30014-2 (hardback)
    ISBN 978-0-374-30015-9 (e-book)
    [1. Running—Fiction.   2. Rats as pets—Fiction.   3. College
choice—Fiction.   4. Family life—Fiction.   5. Best friends—Fiction.
6. Friendship—Fiction.]   I. Title.

PZ7.T64307On 2014
[Fic]—dc23
                                                        2013041345

Farrar Straus Giroux Books for Young Readers may be purchased for business
or promotional use. For information on bulk purchases please contact Macmillan
Corporate and Premium Sales Department at (800) 221-7945 x5442 or
by email at specialmarkets@macmillan.com.

For my editor, Wes Adams,
who asked me to write this book
(and said I could do it)

PART
ONE

I pumped my arms and covered ground with almost no effort. I was Superman. I was Nike—not the shoe company, but the winged goddess of victory. I could practically hear Bruce singing that tramps like us, baby—well, you know.

For one and a half blocks. That's the part he left out. We may have been born to run—but not very far. After two blocks, everything started to hurt. I couldn't get enough air and each leg weighed about eight hundred pounds. Great Lake–sized puddles lurked at every corner and I stepped in all of them. When I tried to leap across, I landed—*splat!*—in the deepest part.

I hadn't expected to see so many people out on this dreary holiday morning. It took only a few minutes for me to realize my New Year's resolution was typical, ordinary, and uninspired—just like me.

The boulevard was buzzing with runners, all trucking along in their tight tights and sporty vests, their long-sleeved shirts with the names of marathons or colleges or clothing brands plastered across the front, their baseball hats from professional football teams and their nondescript black beanies. Some had on backpacks and belts studded with water bottles, as if they were going to be traveling for days. Some people ran alone, and some were in groups. Those in groups chatted as if they were using no more energy than it would take to hoist a latte to their lips. When they came toward me they'd nod and raise a gloved hand.

Which reminded me I was not invisible. I hadn't realized—when I squeezed into the jeggings my mother had bought me years ago (but that I only got to wear to school twice before my best friend, Jenni, told me they were already tragically unhip), donned a long-sleeved T-shirt from an unfortunate family trip to Disney World, and layered on one of my dad's plain old slightly tatty sweatshirts—the superpower I would most want when I set out for my first run would be invisibility.

Each time someone ran past from behind, splattering me with dirty sidewalk water, I straightened up, went a little faster, and tried to hide how hard I was breathing.

And each time someone came toward me I'd look up only for a second, raise a paw in acknowledgment, and think: Don't look at me. Please don't look at me.

My feet hurt because I had secretly borrowed a pair of never-worn, slightly too-small running shoes I found in my mom's shoe room. Yes, my mother has a room just for her shoes. Other people might call it a closet. But then, as Dad likes to point out, other people live in houses with less acreage than the space dedicated to my mother's footwear. She's a material girl, my mom, a doctor who earns enough jack to pay for everything she needs and wants, and a bunch of things that I neither need nor want.

My eyes never stopped watering and I had to constantly wipe my face with my sleeve. I'm sure I looked like I was sobbing throughout the whole thing. It might have been the wind, or maybe I was really crying.

My calves cramped up and I felt dizzy. On the other side of the street I could see a huddle of teens smoking cigarettes. Or something. They yelled an insult, or maybe it was just a whoop, a holler, and I thought again: Make me invisible.

My feet were furious. It felt like my arches had flattened into the shoes. Some jerks drove by in a pickup truck adorned with a Confederate flag and honked their horn. It scared me so much I jumped and landed funny and that made my feet hurt more. I wanted to scream, *Go back to your cave, you howling trolls*, but I didn't say anything.

Then came the panting. I was breathing like a prank caller. My arms were so heavy I could hardly swing them.

And then a guy with long legs, floppy hair, and a dog that looked like Toto with trashy blond highlights passed me.

Hear this, people: I got passed by a dog who was off to see the Wizard. The little dude trotted *fast* on his abbreviated limbs. He held his head high—as high as you could hold a head on legs only about four inches tall. He wore a harness with a camo design, and his leash had rhinestones on it. His mini-legs were going like crazy.

The guy took graceful strides and did not seem like

someone who would have a little dog dressed in camo at the end of a sparkly leash. Toto dogs go with blue-haired old ladies who smell like Cashmere Bouquet body powder and maybe the faintest hint of pee. People and their animals usually look right together. These two didn't.

The guy was around my age. He was attractive. He was so attractive Jenni, a small girl of big appetites, would have referred to him as a tasty morsel. He glided along, his head straight, his arms tucked in neat by his sides.

I struggled to try to keep up with them and did. For about ten seconds. Then they pulled away.

I had been chilly when I left the house, but my body soon *equilibrated* (yes, I paid attention in honors chem), and I sweated through my layers. I stopped for a second to wrestle out of the sweatshirt and tie it around my waist, and looked up to see another pair of runners coming toward me, a guy and a girl. The girl had her hair pulled into a long ponytail and as she ran it swung from side to side, a blond metronome. She was smiling and he was smiling too and he said something and she laughed and she turned and socked the guy with a playful punch to the belly, and he bent over—all while they were still running—and when he stood up straight again I saw the sweatshirt he wore.

It said, "YALE."

The burn rose from my stomach and settled in my throat. I could feel my face flush. I choked up.

The happy couple passed without a wave, without even noticing me, and I thought: Right. In some ways, I am invisible. I am nothing.

I slowed to a walk. My nose was full of snot and I didn't have a tissue. I felt like throwing up. On this day, January 1, I had kept my New Year's resolution and gone for my first run ever.

It was over in eight minutes.

For about seven and a half of those minutes, around 450 seconds, when I had been concentrating on running—on how much my body hurt, on what other people saw when they looked at me, and even on wondering what that hot guy was doing with a Toto dog—I had been able to forget that I, Alice Evelyn Davis, top student in my class at Charleston High School, champion taker of standardized tests, favorite of teachers, and only child of two achievement-focused parents, had been rejected Early Action from Yale University, the only college I ever wanted to go to.

2

When I got home, I said to Walter, "That sucked."

He opened one eye. Then closed it again.

"Maybe I should have picked something easier, like, I don't know, learning to juggle razor blades. Or trying to solve Fermat's last theorem."

Walter sat up. He shook himself and yawned, stretched one hand way out in front of him and flipped it down at the wrist.

"And don't tell me it will get better the more I do it," I warned as I stripped out of my jeggings and freed myself from the T-shirt now pasted to me like one of those skin-treatment masks Jenni uses that makes her look like the Wicked Witch of the West.

"I don't think this is going to get any better, Walter, and I'm not really sure I want to keep doing it. And by the way, when you flick your wrist like that you look kind of effeminate. Not that there's anything wrong with that."

I thought I saw skepticism on Walter's face. Then I remembered he is the least skeptical guy I know. His concern, I soon saw, was not about my pathetic attempt at running, but had to do with his own state of cleanliness. He had the determined look he gets when he thinks he's dirty. Immediately he started washing. He licked both of his hands—dainty little stars, four impossibly tiny fingers and the merest stub of a thumb—and used them to pull his ears down and scrub.

Lick, pull, scrub.

Sometimes he'll sit there holding his ear in his hands, as if he's just remembered an important idea and needs time to think about it.

"Me too," I said, and walked into the bathroom to turn on the shower.

In case you're wondering, Walter is a rat. These days, he's also pretty much my only reason for living, other than Jenni. He's mostly white, with a black hood on his head, in the middle of which is a perfect white diamond. He has a gorgeous line of black splotches down his back. His fur is glossy and silken, and his long whiskers tickle when he gives me a kiss, which he likes to do, and which I like him to do, but not in any kind of pervy way.

Walter has a long, *utilitarian* (SAT word meaning "designed to be useful or practical rather than attractive") tail that I find adorable. But it grosses some people out. Though it has a smattering of hairs on it, it's mostly naked. I have a theory that people's unreasonable and bigoted fear of rats has something to do with the tail, and that has something to do with penises.

Not sure.

All I know is that the rat-o-phobes tend to focus on the tail. That and the plague. Which is ridiculous.

When the rat-haters mention the plague I feel compelled to point out that rats did not cause or carry the plague. Fleas did. The fleas bit the rats, transmitted the virus (that killed the rats), and then jumped onto humans to bite and kill them. Rats were innocent victims, people. And, by the way, lots of animals carry plague, even cute furry-tailed ones. Right now, in the western part of the United States, there are more prairie dogs infested with plague than there were afflicted rats during the Black Death. (I wrote a term paper on this for biology freshman year and really got into it.)

Though Walter grooms himself endlessly, making sure every hair is in place, he tends to neglect the flexible extension of his backbone.

We've had many discussions about tail hygiene. "Walter," I say, "you must attend to your tail. You are giving the rat-haters ammo." But I haven't seen a lot of progress on his part. So every couple of weeks I give him a bath in the sink. He often poops when he hits the water and will not listen to reason about how completely disgusting that is. I scrub his tail and shampoo and condition the rest of him.

Afterward I tell him he looks like a drowned rat. I rub him down with a washcloth and then roll him up in it and turn him into a little vermin burrito. Then I blow-dry him on a low setting until he's fluffy. "You're no longer a dirty varmint," I say, and he looks up at me with the face of love. Then he starts licking himself again.

Yes, the man of my dreams is the size of a salami. I know there are stereotypes about kids who have rats: They are the loners. They are the misunderstood. They are the weirdos who use their animals as freak flags. But honestly, the reason most folks have rats is because they're fantastic companions, especially when you consider the list of other "pocket pets":

1. Hamsters: Aggressive little a-holes who, when they're not sleeping, which they do for about twenty-three hours a day, will bite you and draw blood.
2. Gerbils: The neurotic Ben Stillers of the rodent world, all jerky movements and self-doubt.
3. Guinea pigs: Stupid. I know you're not supposed to say things like this, that not everyone can be in the gifted and talented program, but, well, not everyone can. Some of these guys even look dumb, with hair that grows in different directions and seems to need product. And they make creepy noises.
4. Ferrets: Freaking stinky. Even if you de-nasty them by surgically removing their scent glands, they still smell musky and rank. Plus, they kind of look like snakes with fur.
5. Rabbits: High maintenance. You have to feed them salad every day and then they poop out

these round pellets that look like something animals should eat and not expel. And guess what? They do eat them! *Coprophagy* ("eating feces"). Rabbits have supersoft fur but don't like to be held, which strikes me as obnoxious.

6. Mice: I have to admit to a fondness for mice. When you see a whole bunch of them in a cage in the pet store, it looks like a city. Everyone's on the move. Everyone's busy. Sometimes there will be three or four guys on a wheel running in one direction and another guy scrambling the other way, and that guy ends up riding around upside down and it looks like they're all having a blast. Mice have a lot going on. But cool as they are, they're not rats.

Rats are the smartest, most social, and all-around best pet. If you don't believe me, ask a veterinarian or someone who works in a laboratory. They all say the same thing: rats are the best small mammals.

And Walter is the best of the best small mammals ever. He's clever and sweet and loving. He has a great sense of humor and an even deeper well of empathy. He was on my lap last month when I found out I had been rejected—not even deferred—Early Action from my dream school.

I sat at the computer, stunned. Walter crawled up my shirt and nestled on my neck, licking the tears from my face. As I stared at the screen, I could picture the word stamped in red on my application and felt like it was now tattooed across my forehead.

Alice Evelyn Davis = REJECT.

I am unaccustomed to not getting the things I want.

As the sole offspring of two conspicuously consuming professionals *riddled* ("filled or permeated with some-thing unpleasant") with guilt about working too much and not paying enough attention to their precious child, I am often the beneficiary of bouts of excessive spending. For the record, I get plenty of attention, often more than I want. But my mother likes everything to be perfect, including me. So my room, the entire third floor of our house, is a luxury suite far too fancy for a seventeen-year-old girl.

It's not that I'm not grateful for all the ways my life is made cushy and nice by my parents—okay, by my mother; my father would be happy living in a hovel as long as he had a bunch of books and a *New York Times* crossword puzzle on his iPad—but to be honest, I just don't care that much about stuff. Maybe that's because I have so much of it.

I realize that this is a first-world problem. While my parents aren't private-jet rich or own-a-pied-à-terre-in-Manhattan rich, the fact is, they have a lot of coin. They make up for it by being extra-liberal in their politics and doing charitable giving. A lot of dough still comes my way. Unlike many kids from my school, including Jenni, I won't have to worry about being able to pay for college. I just have to worry about not getting in anywhere I've applied.

My bedroom has a big four-poster bed covered with a soft blue-and-white Egyptian-cotton quilt and a ridiculous number of pillows. What I've gathered from my mother's "shelter porn" magazines is that the richer someone is, the more pillows of different sizes and shapes she has on her bed.

I also have a whole other space with two big couches positioned at a ninety-degree angle and a marble coffee table between them. I'm supposed to use coasters if I put a drink down on the fancy table. Instead, I don't use it. The couches face a huge flat-screen TV hung on the wall, which I can see perfectly well from my bed so I rarely sit in the sitting area. The couch closest to my bed is where Jenni sleeps when she stays over, which she does a lot. She hunkers down in this old red flannel sleeping bag with drawings of cowboys on it. It belonged to Dad when he was a kid. He refused to throw it out, even though Mom threatened to divorce him if he kept bringing it downstairs. I was happy to rescue it, and Jenni loves sleeping among the eternally young boys who wear chaps and throw lassos.

I have bookcases filled with books I've read and reread a zillion times and dressers crammed with clothes I never wear. A large number of the books used to be my dad's. For years I've been raiding his shelves and *appropriating* ("taking something for one's own use, especially without the owner's permission") his collection. The clothes come from my mother's shopping jags. Some still have price tags on them. Mom thinks if she finds a hundred-and-fifty-dollar sweater for me and buys it for half price, she's saved money. I try to tell her I don't want any more clothes, but she doesn't listen. We end up doing a purge once a year and all these brand-new purchases go to Value Village, and she writes it off as a tax deduction. I've seen kids at school wearing the clothes we dropped off.

My closet has built-in shelves for sweaters and jeans and cubbyholes for shoes. It also has in it a big ugly gold velour overstuffed armchair from our old house. My mother tried to get rid of it and I pitched a fit. After my too-many-pillowed bed, it's my second-favorite place to read.

My desk is in a nook by the bay window and I have a chair that's supposed to be good for your back named after the designer who came up with it and convinced people to spend a bucketload of money on something not very attractive.

Attached to my room is a bathroom with a heated marble floor, a Jacuzzi tub I never use, and a shower I do. The shower is actually great; it attacks you with streams of water from all sides. And, because Mom did a tour of Europe after college and became smitten with French bathrooms, there is a bidet.

If you don't know what this is, you probably don't want to know. Here's a hint: sometimes I threaten to give Walter a bath in the bidet because it's meant for those with dirty tails.

Walter has a cage, of course, a three-story deluxe playhouse. Like me, he thinks his accommodations are a waste of space and spends most of his time in the tiny sleeping hut Jenni made for him. When I'm home, we have an open-door policy, and he's welcome to go wherever he wants. The great thing about a room this big is that during free-range-rodent time, Walter gets plenty of exercise and can stimulate his brain with explorations. However, he usually wants to be where I am.

Most often, I am in the chair in my closet or in bed, reading, or with my laptop looking up stuff or playing Snood. I play a lot of Snood even though it's not that much fun. I'll play a few games, and forty-five minutes later, I tell myself I'll just play one more.

And then I play another.

And another.

It's hard to quit once I've started. These days, I haven't done much reading or looking stuff up. Snood is about all I'm good for.

Last year Mom kept saying that computer games don't count as extracurricular activities on college applications. I hate it when she's right.

Walter is happy to sleep on my shoulder or my chest, but what he likes most is when I'm lying down and my legs are straight out in front of me and he can burrow in between them right above my knees. He has a tendency to nibble on my jeans, and I have tons of tiny holes in my favorite pair. When Mom complains, I remind her people pay a lot of money for jeans with holes in them. I tell her I might rent Walter out to the high-end designers she likes to support. It would be good for him to have a job, I say.

Mom just lets out a big sigh when I say stuff like that

and shakes her head to remind me that I am not the perfect daughter she was hoping for.

Walter trails me to the bathroom. He usually follows me around when he's not in a deep, curled-up sleep. He's more doglike than many dogs. He does tricks. He can push a marble around the floor with his nose and can climb anything. He comes when you call him. He has a special dance he does for broccoli, a joyous twirling, circling ballet of love. He's a rat of many talents. If there were a gifted-and-talented school for rodents, Walter would be the valedictorian.

3

That first run was so depressing, and being reminded about Yale was so icky, that I stayed in the shower for a long time, probably in the misguided if unconscious belief that I could wash some of the shame off.

Didn't work.

But I stayed in so long Walter decided to check up on me. When I dropped the soap I saw him standing on his back feet with his paws against the glass of the shower stall. He left tiny handprints in the steam. Looking at him made me feel better. I begged him to answer the question, "How can anyone be so cute and wonderful?"

I named Walter after our family friend Walter.

Not after him in the sense of paying tribute, but more because I thought he would find it annoying. I like to annoy him and he likes it when I annoy him. I call Walter the man *Walter-the-Man* and Walter the rat *Walter*.

Walter-the-Man is a lawyer who works at the same law firm as my dad. He lives down the street. He eats at our house most weekends and many weekday nights and has done ever since I can remember. He's usually parked in front of our TV watching college basketball, especially

Duke, which he follows with a fervor that knows no bounds or reason—or football or baseball or golf or Wiffle ball—and drinking a beer.

Walter-the-Man is like a human piece of furniture, comfortably overstuffed like my closet chair, and like my chair, a bit worn down. He spends what little vacation time he takes going to see the Barenaked Ladies or the Dave Matthews Band.

I tell him it's kind of sad, a middle-aged man traveling around the country to hear middle-aged men sing.

He tells me nothing's less appealing than a jaded teen.

Sometimes, when I say something sassy, Walter-the-Man will secretly flip me the bird. I'll respond by shaking both my middle fingers at him and we keep this up until we're afraid that one of my parents will see us. Then we'll giggle and Mom will say, "What? What's so funny?" and Walter-the-Man will say, "Nothing. Alice and I were just discussing the trade imbalance with China and the federal-budget deficit."

Walter-the-Man was in a long-distance relationship with a woman named Deborah for a couple years. I never met her and they broke up in the spring of my freshman year, though they have remained friends. She is dean of admissions at some university in North Carolina. They saw each other infrequently but apparently talked on the phone for hours. Walter spent a lot of time telling us her stories "from the front lines of the bloody college-admissions battle." He'd tell them in a news-announcer voice.

Last year, when I had to pretend to be interested in

schools other than Yale, Walter-the-Man offered to have Deborah talk to me and give me some advice.

I didn't think I needed any. All the crazy things he told us about what the students and parents did to get in had nothing to do with me. Because:

1. I am the top student at my high school.
2. My SAT scores are 780, 800, and 800.
3. I have high 700s and a few 800s on my SAT IIs.
4. I am a National Merit Semifinalist.
5. I've taken the handful of AP classes offered by my school and got 5's on the AP tests.

Most kids from our school who go to college—and not all that many do—end up at one of the state universities and many of them start out at a community college. The National Honor Society kids go to the U.

Hardly anyone applies to fancy-pants colleges, but both my parents grew up in New York City and went to Bowdoin, a dinky private college in Maine, which is where they met. They both have graduate degrees from Duke. They aren't snobby or anything, but they have told me since I can remember that while they have chosen to live here, I should probably go some place more *urbane* ("refined") for college.

I figured you couldn't get more urbane than Yale, one of the oldest schools in one of the oldest states in the country. But that wasn't the reason I first got interested in it.

My favorite book is the tattered copy of *The Norton Anthology of Poetry* Dad used in college. Sometimes he and I sit around and read poems aloud and then analyze them. I know how nerdy that makes me sound, but really, it's what I like to do. Dad likes it too, and I like to make him happy. We especially love Wallace Stevens and Emily Dickinson and Robert Frost and Theodore Roethke. I adore Sylvia Plath.

I was obsessed with *The Bell Jar* for a while and asked my family to call me Esther, but it didn't stick. Dad doesn't love old Sylvia. She's a tad too nutty for him, he says.

Once I noticed how many poets had gone to Yale, I decided that's where I would go to college. This was in the days when I thought I might want to write poetry. I had a great English teacher in eighth grade, Mr. Brooks, and he made me think I could be a poet. I've since given up on that and am happy just to read poetry and talk about it with Dad and Ms. Chan, my English teacher this year, but the Yale part stayed with me.

It was all set: I did really well in school; I'd apply to Yale and go there.

In my mind, it was a done deal. What did I have to worry about?

After Walter-the-Man broke up with Deborah, he dated Sage, a cosmetician twenty-five years his junior. Mom kept telling him what an idiot he was, that he needed to grow the hell up, that Deborah had been his perfect match, that he wasn't going to do better.

He responded by telling my mother she needed a deeper hair conditioner and she might want to consider a French manicure because her fingers looked kind of stubby. Then he gave her a gift certificate to a day spa. My mother loves pampering and it stopped her from nagging Walter-the-Man about ditching Deborah. For about fifteen minutes.

When he started seeing Chef Susan, Walter-the-Man began to comment on Dad's cooking. He'd say, "Chef Susan uses pancetta and porcini in her omelets." I had to look up both of those things and found out Chef Susan made eggs with bacon and mushrooms—big whoop.

He said things like, "Chef Susan thinks copper pots give better temperature control than those Le Creusets you use."

Dad finally told Walter-the-Man he could go eat Chef Susan's food if it was so great, but when he had dinner with us, he might consider developing an interest in the weather.

Not long afterward, a copper pot appeared on my dad's stove. When Dad tried to thank him, Walter-the-Man said, "I have no idea what you're talking about, Matt."

Walter-the-Man likes to try to use me as his servant. From his (GO DUKE!) basketball/football/volleyball/golf/shuffleboard-watching post in front of our TV he'll wave an empty bottle at me and say, "Hey, Alice, go fetch me another beer."

I'll say, "No, sir, Walter-the-Man, I'm not your retriever. You can fetch your own dang beer. And don't be asking me to do your laundry or cook your meals or clean your toilet, either. If you want a maid, bucko, pay for one."

But I'll always go into the kitchen and get him another beer.

Walter-the-Man may be a pain in the butt, but he's our pain in the butt.

4

A big mistake you can make with a New Year's resolution is to tell people about it, especially people who will remember and ask you how it's going. They're trying to be helpful, though sometimes you feel like you're being bullied by your own good intentions.

Of course I told Jenni about my resolution, since it was her idea to make resolutions in the first place, and also because if you don't tell your best friend about something, it's like it doesn't exist. That's part of what it means to have a best friend: you have a warehouse for all your stray thoughts, which, if you keep them in your head, don't seem as real as they do when you hear them come out of your mouth.

Jenni never forgets one single thing. We've been friends for more than a decade and although we're different in lots of ways, she knows me better than anyone. She'll remember what I wore the time we went bowling with these skeevy guys from Morgantown who tried to get us to eat mushrooms—not the kind you put in omelets—and she'll remember what flavor birthday cake I've had every year since we were six. She'll remember the time I drank a bunch of Southern Comfort and she had to hold my hair back while I puked and said I was never going to drink alcohol again, something I think about each time I drink alcohol, but she never mentions. She'll remember I said I didn't want to go to college still a virgin, but she doesn't point out I've never even kissed a boy.

She doesn't bring these things up to use against me, as some bad friends would, but instead waits for me to mention something or ask her a question: What was the name of that restaurant we went to that time in New York City? Where did I first have tiramisu? And then she'll tell me. So she's not only a storeroom for random thoughts but also the historian of my life.

A few nights before New Year's Eve, Jenni and I were at my house.

I had been complaining about my Yale rejection. Which was pretty much the only thing I'd talked or thought about for the previous two weeks. Jenni had been trying to comfort me, but like everyone else, she was so surprised I had been rejected she didn't know what to say except that they were making a big mistake. I'd given up trying to argue.

Jenni didn't understand why Yale was such a big deal to me, since no one from her family had even gone to college.

Jenni didn't talk about her plans for next year and I avoided asking. I didn't want to pressure her and make her feel bad if she chose not to go, which was kind of what I expected.

Instead, I kept trying to make her see what a failure

I was and that I probably wouldn't get in anywhere else. But she loves me too much to see my flaws, and she indulges me when I spend hours pointing out these very same flaws. Jenni just kept saying, "They're making a big mistake. They'll be sorry when you're interviewed by Oprah."

That night my parents went out to a holiday party. I had to beg them to go. Mom threatened to cancel because she was worried about me.

For two weeks I'd been saying I wanted to stick my head in the oven.

For two weeks I had barked and snarled at everyone who wasn't Walter.

I was miserable for darned sure, but I wasn't suicidal.

When I said I wanted to stick my head in the oven it was a joke. Black humor, people. But no one thought I was in a joke-making frame of mind.

I had to remind my mother we had an electric oven and if I tried to pull a Sylvia Plath, all I'd manage was to singe my hair and eyebrows off.

Still, before my parents went out I overheard Mom tell Jenni to keep an eye on me. Which is kind of funny, since Jenni does that all the time anyway. It's kind of her job. Just like my job is to make a lot of obnoxious comments. And to make her believe in herself more. For such an amazing person, Jenni can be a little insecure.

Jenni and I lay on my bed with a buffet of snack bags between us. Walter was on bed patrol, sniffing around and peering over the edge to make sure the perimeter was secure. Then he walked into a bag of Ritz Bits.

"Hey," said Jenni. "He's in the bag." She looked a little disgusted, though it's not like she hasn't seen him do this kind of thing seven thousand times.

Walter wasn't, technically, in the bag. Only his front end was. On a search-and-destroy mission, he grabbed a Ritz Bits, backed out of the bag, and retreated to my lap, where he perched to disarm it with his teeth.

"Okay," said Jenni. "It's time to resolve."

"Resolve what?"

"Resolve what we're going to do better next year. New Year's is coming, or did you forget because you don't approve of a holiday that's all about getting drunk and making noise."

It's true. I don't like New Year's Eve. It's noisy and unruly and usually cold.

Plus, there's no good candy. The best holidays involve candy. I'm a big fan of Christmas, even though my family doesn't celebrate it, because there's so much good stuff to eat. Hanukah's pretty lame in comparison. Those gold chocolate coins we get for playing dreidel taste like poop medicine.

This year, I was too *dejected* ("sad and depressed") to help Jenni bake Christmas cookies, which is something we always do. She likes to give them out to everyone she knows and even some people she doesn't know that well, like our UPS driver and the secretaries at school.

As far as holidays go, Halloween is tops in my book, except for the whole costume part. I try to be strategic about gathering a year's supply of Indian corn because it's seasonal, and even then, it comes only in small bags. If you get the larger bags of Autumn Mix, you end up with a few Indian corns, a lot of regular old candy corn, and a bunch of nasty pumpkins.

I can't stand the pumpkins so I make Jenni eat them. She likes to point out they're made of exactly the same stuff as candy corn so why don't I like them?

"BECAUSE THEY TASTE COMPLETELY DIFFER-ENT!" I have to gently remind her.

Jenni doesn't understand how shapes affect taste. She also doesn't understand the Peeps hierarchy.

It's a happy day when Easter Peeps make their annual appearance at the grocery store. I only like the yellow chicks, which must be eaten stale—or frozen, if you don't have the time to leave them out—and you have to nibble the butt first and then bite off the head. The pink bunnies are okay, but everything else in Peeps-dom is a wannabe.

Don't get me started on the purples and the blues.

Or on Peeps for other holidays. That's just wrong.

I'd gotten so worked up thinking about candy I managed to forget, for a few minutes, that my future career might be ringing up Peeps at a grocery store and asking, "Paper or plastic?"

"Resolution," said Jenni. "New Year's. Now."

I pounded my right fist on my heart and said, "I hereby

resolve to be more like Walter," which was, when you think about it, not a half-bad resolution.

"Alice," Jenni said.

I said, "Walter is always in a good mood. He's curious and playful and interested in others. He's loyal and faithful and has a great sense of humor. He's open to new things and never bites anyone. He eats when he's hungry, and when he's full, instead of stuffing his face until he needs to go lie down, he stashes the leftovers. Now, it might be better if he didn't store them in the far corners of the closet or under the bed, since sometimes he forgets about the piles and they start to rot and stink, and Mom gets all, 'You can't let that rat spread food all over the house,' and I have to clean up after him, but it's a good policy in case we ever run out of food. You can't fault someone for preparing for a rainy day."

I stopped for a minute to poke Walter in the belly. He grabbed my digit with both of his tiny four-fingered hands and brought it to his mouth and licked it.

"And," I continued, "Walter would not have been rejected from the one school he wanted to go to. He's never failed at anything in his life. And he loves me even though I'm a loser."

"Alice, knock it off already. You are so far from being a loser that if all the losers in the world had a gigantic party, you wouldn't even make it to the C-list. Until two weeks ago, you had never failed at anything in your life. Come on, I think we should do this. Let's each think of something."

"You don't think Walter is worthy of emulation?" I can get defensive on Walter's behalf, since there has been such a long history of bigoted persecution against his species.

"No, Alice, I am not saying anything bad about Walter. You know I like Walter, and I know you love him and, yes, I agree, he is a model citizen in many ways. You're right: everyone should try to be more like Walter."

She offered him a Mini Oreo, which is okay for rats to eat since:

1. Chocolate is not toxic for rats the way it is for dogs.
2. I'm not sure there's any chocolate in an Oreo.
3. I don't allow anything in my room that might be dangerous for rats.

Walter held it with his hands at nine and three, like a perfect driver's-ed student, and began munching away in careful bites.

"What I'm saying, though," Jenni continued, "is I think we need to find a way to get you to move on."

"Okay, how about if I resolve to get rejected from more colleges? Oops. Never mind. That's going to happen anyway."

Right after I got the bad news from Yale, I knew I had to submit applications to other schools. The guidance counselor, who never remembered my name, was no help.

She'd told me I had zero chance of getting into Yale in

the first place and that I was crazy to even try. No one from our school had ever gone there, she said, and she advised me to apply to the honors college at the U. My English teacher, Ms. Chan, and Mr. Bergmann, my biology teacher, who really liked my paper on the plagued prairie dogs, had encouraged me and volunteered to write letters of recommendation. They both said that I was the best student they'd had in all their years of teaching.

For the first week after Rejection Day I did nothing.

Then I cut-and-pasted my personal statement into the Common Application form and sent it to a bunch of other colleges.

I spent very little time on the supplemental essays. Instead of writing draft after draft the way I did for the short-answer questions on my Yale application, I just typed them in and sent them off.

Walter had crawled up to perch on my shoulder and take a nap. As Jenni popped a handful of Mini Oreos into her mouth I said, "Maybe I could get a job as a spokesperson for the Rejected throughout the world. I could give speeches on the different ways to cry after you've been rejected. I could do a YouTube video showing the silent tears, the sniffling, breathy hiccuping gasps, the all-out sobs. I could be the poster child for rejection. I could teach other kids how to wallow."

Jenni nodded and said, "Yeah, you've become a real expert on wallowing. I think you need to find something else to focus on. Before your best friend and your rat get sick of listening to you whine. A hobby. A project!"

She clapped her hands. Jenni is the queen of projects.

"You sound too much like Mom for me to want to talk to you," I said, and got up.

All year long Mom had been telling me to relax, not stress out so much, take it easy, and I was like, "Oh really? You want me to sit around and smoke pot all day and drink Red Bull and grain alcohol all night like the kids in my school who will end up spending their post-graduation days inquiring, 'Do you want cheese on that?'"

Relax? Has she never met me? I have never been a *relax* kind of kid. Cripes.

And it's not like my mother is some kind of shiny role model of Zen-ed-out calm. Most mornings she leaves for the office before I get up. She spends long days chopping out cancerous moles and shooting wrinkle-paralyzing poison into the foreheads of wealthy women. Some days she puffs up their lips with the medical equivalent of Silly Putty.

My mother injects Botox into her own face the way other people put on makeup. There's always a bottle of it in the fridge. As soon as her forehead starts to move, she's in the bathroom with a needle. She says it's important that patients see her as an example.

My mother thinks a lot about being an example.

She has to be the best at everything. She makes Scrabble into a blood sport. She once got injured in a yoga class because her teacher commended her for being flexible. She said, "Oh yeah? Watch this!" and tried to put her leg behind her head and ended up tearing her hamstring.

About three times a week after dinner, as I head upstairs to lie in my bed with Walter and read, Mom and I enact the same scene.

"Alice, why don't you go outside and get some exercise?"

"Because I don't feel like it. I'm going upstairs to read."

"You're always reading. You need to move around more. You need to use your muscles, to get out there and do something."

"I am doing something. Reading."

"Something physical. Why don't you try out for the tennis team?"

"I don't like tennis. And, Mom, I don't like swimming. And I don't like soccer. And I don't like volleyball, basketball, or softball. I don't like to be in any situation in which a projectile comes flying toward my head, and I don't like team sports."

"But it would be good for you. You spend so much time alone."

"No, *Mom*," I say, using her name in italics the way she does mine when she is trying to convey *I am making an important point*. "I have Walter. And Jenni, when she's not with Kyle."

"It's wonderful that you and Jenni are so close, but really, I think it would be good if you had more than one friend."

At that point, I get annoyed and may occasionally raise my voice. Okay, so in truth, I end up shouting at her: "AND WALTER, Mom. I have Walter."

"Yes, you do have Walter."

Some nights she gives up, but other nights she rallies and keeps going: "How about theater? You loved theater in middle school. I know they are doing a musical this spring. Jenni's designing costumes for it. You have a beautiful voice."

"I am not doing theater anymore, especially not a musical. I refuse to participate in something where people, instead of talking like normal humans, all of a sudden start singing and dancing. You may not have noticed but life isn't like that."

"What about debate? You do like to argue."

"No I don't."

"Of course you do. Oh—I get it. Ha-ha."

"No you don't."

"Okay, Alice, enough."

"Look," I say, "I'd just like to point out that most parents wouldn't complain about a kid who loves school, is at the top of her class, doesn't get into trouble, and likes to stay home and read."

Then Mom says, "Fine."

And I say, "Fine."

And she goes back to reading her magazine and turns the pages really loudly.

The more she nags, the more comfy my butt feels in the chair. For a smart woman, my mother is not very *savvy* ("perceptive, shrewd"—easy word, but hard to spell because two *v*'s in a row look weird) about motivation. Lately it seems like she's been enlisting Jenni to side with her. They have been doing more stuff together this year, shopping

34

and messing around with hair products and makeup. I would be jealous except:

1. It gets Mom off my back.
2. Jenni is like a sister to me.
3. Jenni's mom died when we were little and I'm happy to share mine with her.

While I often get annoyed with my mother and treat her kind of badly, I am much more careful with Jenni.

So on that night, as we crept toward the end of the year of my rejection and greatest failure and toward a new one that offered who knew what, after she told me I needed to stop whining and get a project, I felt bad for snapping at her.

Another of the things a best friend does is call you on your crap.

So I said, "I'm getting another glass of milk. Refill?"

"Yes, please," she said, and when she handed me her glass I saw she was afraid she'd upset me, so I said, "Don't worry about it. I'll be back in a nanosecond. Keep an eye on my baby boy."

Walter, at that point, was exploring the hills and hollows made by the quilt on my bed.

"Come here, Walt, little buddy," I heard Jenni say to him as I went downstairs.

5

Jenni has lots of hobbies and projects.

She sews.

She designs and makes most of her clothes. What she doesn't make she gets from my mother and me. We have the Jenni Sack, a big cloth bag where we put the clothes we no longer want, which for my mother is pretty much anything after she's worn it once, and for me is pretty much everything Mom buys me. A few times a year Jenni grabs the sack and takes it home to her sewing room. The things that don't fit her she alters; the things she isn't crazy about she transforms. She can turn a dress into a shirt, a pair of pants into capris. We have logged serious hours watching *Project Runway* and I bet someday, if she wants to, Jenni could be a contestant. She could even win. We love Tim Gunn so much. Sometimes one of us will walk into a room with our left arm cocked at a ninety-degree angle and say, "Designers! How are we doing? Gather around!"

Jenni also knits.

She learned to knit from her mom, who had been our house cleaner. Starting when we were six, they would come over twice a week and Jenni and I got to be best friends.

Then her mom got sick.

She passed away when we were ten.

Not long after that, Jenni's sister got pregnant, dropped out of school, and moved to Kentucky. Her dad works for a company that cuts down trees for the coal mines. Then he comes home and drinks too much or goes to an AA meeting, depending on whether he's off the wagon or on.

Jenni often says that without me, without my family, she would be lost. She says she doesn't know what would have happened to her after her mom died. She loves that I encourage her to try new things, even when it can make her a smidge uncomfortable, and that I come up with ideas and point out stuff that would never occur to her.

She spends a lot of time at our house and joins us on family vacations. In addition to clothes, Mom always gives Jenni the free samples she picks up from the Chanel and Estée Lauder counters. Often when she sees something Jenni would like, a lip gloss or eye shadow or face powder, Mom will buy it. She tells Jenni it was a mistake—the wrong color for her and she's going to throw it away if Jenni doesn't want it.

Jenni can get twitchy about accepting too much from our family and says she hates being a charity case. Of course, none of us think of her like that. I've wondered whether she tries to be extra nice and helpful all the time because she feels indebted. But then I realize no, that's just who she is. She's unselfish to a fault and doesn't like to be the center of attention. She deflects conversation away from herself—so much so it can be hard to get her to talk about what's on her mind.

Sometimes, though, when she's knitting, Jenni will say, "I miss her, Al."

I know she's thinking about her mom, the person who taught her to knit, and I'll say, "I know," and "I'm so sorry."

She'll start crying, and I'll just hold her hand and stroke her hair and wait until she's breathing normally again, and then I'll give her a tissue and talk about what she's knitting. I'll try to be upbeat and say, in my best Tim Gunn voice, "Make it work!"

Jenni's favorite class at school, the only one she ever gets an A in, is something Walter-the-Man refers to as shop class.

"No, Walter-the-Man," I say, "shop class is the kind of thing my mother would teach. What Jenni likes is called Machinery and Engineering." That's where she learns stuff like woodworking, architectural drafting, and how to solder circuits. She made Walter's sleeping hut after we spent hours discussing the design. After that, in Machinery and Engineering II, she learned how to weld—it was Jenni and five guys wearing face masks wielding an acetylene torch. She made me a metal sculpture of a rat.

Unlike Jenni, the only thing I am good at is school. I've never gotten anything less than an A and I always have my papers done days or weeks before they are due. Sometimes, if I do them too early and leave them lying around when Walter is on the prowl, the corners get nib-bled.

When I give Ms. Chan a paper that has no teeth marks, she says, "What? Not good enough for Walter?"

The only other person who seems to like school as much as I do is Sam Malouf. He's my biggest competition for valedictorian, but he's not that good at math so I'm ranked ahead of him. Even though I don't love math as much as I love English and biology and chemistry and physics and history and government, I'm still good at it.

Other than Jenni, I don't really have any close friends. At least, not my own age—or species. Maybe it's because I am an only child, but I've always been more comfortable around grownups and animals than other kids.

Jenni has a group of cheerleaders she sometimes hangs out with. (Did I mention that in addition to being able to make CAD drawings and weld, Jenni is also a Varsity cheerleader?) I call them the Brittanys.

There are three of them: Brittany, Brittney, and Tif-fany.

Jenni is closest friends with Tiffany. Being with them makes me feel geeky and shabby. It's not like I am some disadvantaged kid. I have tons of advantages. Way more than most people. But I just don't fit in at school and I've given up trying.

I wish I could blame it on something other than my personality.

Plus, the Brittanys do this thing girls do that drives me nuts, where all they talk about is how much they suck.

I mean, I may *think* I suck, but I don't talk about it to anyone other than Walter and Jenni.

But when you're with the Brittanys, you'd think they were the biggest losers in the world instead of cheerleaders who rule the school.

One of them will say, "I love your hair like that."

The hair in question will respond, "Oh god, it's a mess. I couldn't make it do anything this morning."

"I like that dress" provokes "It's too small for me. My belly pooches out. It would look better on you."

"You're so pretty!"

"I am not. Look at my hands! I have man hands."

They *parry* ("to wave off a weapon or a blow") compliments the way Captain Jack Sparrow *brandishes* ("to wave or shake") a sword.

The worst is when someone says something nice about a piece of clothing Jenni has made—something I know she's worked hard on and is proud of—and the first thing she does is point out the flaws.

It's like there's this code among girls that *stipulates* ("demands or specifies") no one is supposed to feel good about herself or anything she's done. The game is to say, "No, no, I suck and you're great," and the response has to be, "No, no, I suck," and it goes on and on like this.

But sewing and knitting and cheering and welding are not even Jenni's most important hobbies.

Jenni's main extracurricular activity is being a girlfriend.

Since junior year she's been a girlfriend to Kyle, also known as the stud muffin.

Kyle plays three sports and uses a lot of product in his hair. Everyone thinks he's hot. He barely passes his classes, doesn't always bother to conjugate his verbs when he speaks, and can get loud and obnoxious when he's with his teammates. He's always throwing a bulky arm around Jenni and sort of shaking her and saying, "You're the best, babe." He calls her babe and she doesn't even mind.

What I don't like is that Kyle holds Jenni back. He keeps her from taking chances and trying new things. He just wants her to be his own personal cheerleader.

The problem isn't really the stud muffin, though; it's that Jenni thinks she needs to have a boyfriend, as if she believes there's something missing from her without a guy. Since middle school, she has never been without one. Me, I've never even come close to going on a date.

In the kitchen I refilled our glasses with milk and grabbed more Ritz Bits, the snack favored by discriminating vermin, and more bags of Mini Oreos, Mini Chips Ahoy!, and Nutter Butter Bites.

The minis taste better than the regular-size ones because the ratio of cookie to cream is right, and because everything mini is better.

I love mini-foods, like mini–corn on the cob and mini-muffins, and bonsai, which are mini-trees, and mini-bottles of shampoo, and mini-cars (I want a Mini Cooper but Dad says no way because he thinks they're too small to be safe).

With tiny stuff, imperfections and mistakes aren't as noticeable.

Every day I seem to be more aware of how easy it is to find imperfections and to make mistakes.

When I came back upstairs Jenni and Walter were reading *People*. Well, Jenni was reading and Walter was sitting on the bottom of the magazine, and every time Jenni wanted to turn a page she had to move Walter.

I caught her apologizing to him for the disruption.

Jenni reached out for her glass of milk and I snuggled in next to her. Walter crawled onto my lap and I handed him a chunk of Nutter Butter.

"Okay," I said. "You're right. I do need a hobby."

Jenni flipped another page of *People* and there was this big picture of Jennifer Aniston running. The woman is like, ancient, but she has a body that looks better than— well, better than anyone's. She seemed superstrong and happy.

And suddenly I got an idea.

I paused because I didn't know if this was a good idea and I knew if I said it, I was committing myself. I don't take things like promises or resolutions lightly.

But as much as I hated to admit it, my mother was right: I needed to get outside more.

And Jenni was right: I needed to do something instead of just sitting around complaining about Yale.

Plus, my thighs. My butt.

"I am going to start running."

Jenni's eyes got big for a moment and she blinked a few

times, and then, because she always wants to be positive and supportive, she said, "Great idea, Al!"

It was, I admit, an odd choice. I'm basically lazy. I don't like to sweat. I get annoyed with the rah-rah jocks and am suspicious of anything that smells of team spirit.

But something about that picture of Jennifer Aniston, how she looked so happy and so free, so not like a reject, made me want to try to run.

Plus, her thighs. Her butt.

Jenni said, "Running. Perfect! You can do it whenever you want and you don't have to rely on anyone else. I know how much you hate waiting for other people."

I smiled because Jenni can be, let's say, poky when it comes to getting ready to go out and she tends to show up for things anywhere from fifteen to forty minutes late. Usually it's because she's in the bathroom fixing her makeup.

I've threatened to fine her a quarter for every minute she makes me wait, but she doesn't have that kind of money. I tell her I don't have that kind of time.

We both know it isn't true.

"We'll see how it goes," I said. "I'm not going to tell anyone except you, especially not Mom. So let's don't talk about it."

Jenni zipped her lips with her finger. Walter had his hand on my glass and poked his head into the milk.

"Yes, sweet baby, you can have a sip," I said to him. He stretched down into the glass and lapped up a drop or two.

"Alice, really. Do you think that's a good idea, sharing your milk with him?" She sounded exactly like my mother.

"Yes, Jenni, I do. There's a temple in India that houses twenty thousand rats and the priests feed them bread and milk and it's considered good luck to have food sampled by a rat."

"Do I need to remind you we're not in India?"

"And the Hindu elephant-headed god, Lord Ganesh, rides on a rat."

"Whatevs," said Jenni, no longer sounding like my mother.

"Also, in the Chinese zodiac, the rat kicks off the animal calendar. Those born in the Year of the Rat possess qualities of creativity, honesty, generosity, and ambition."

Coincidentally, I happen to have been born in the Year of the Rat. I didn't know this until after I'd already gotten Walter and started Googling all things ratty. The Chinese New Year doesn't start for another month, and then we'll be in the Year of the Snake.

The Year of the Dragon, the one that's on its way out, breathed fire on me until I nearly shriveled from rejection. I'm really hoping the Snake will be kinder, but I have my doubts; it's hard to think about snakes—who dine on rats—being kind.

Jenni had gone back to leafing through *People* and had landed on a page of photos of Katie Holmes and Suri. She seemed to be trying to memorize Suri's dress. My guess was she was going to try to copy it.

"What's yours?" I asked.

"What's my what?"

"Your New Year's resolution. You said we needed to get serious. It was your idea," I said. "Remember? Like, three minutes ago."

"Oh," she said, "I'm going to stop biting my nails."

I looked at her perfect delicate hands whose too-short nails made them seem human and not doll-like. And I thought: that's too bad.

6

Jenni is the bestest bestie, a supergood BFF. Unfortunately, she is also pretty, and petite, and she makes her own clothes and is a girly-girl who can weld, for Pete's sake. She is one of the nicest, most patient people you could ever meet.

Nothing wrong with being pretty and petite and nice, I know. Did I mention she has a perfect, heart-shaped butt?

And straight white teeth?

And hair the color mine would be if it got to live on a tropical island all the time? Hair that's silky, not hay-like. I swear to god I've had horses try to eat my hair, and who could blame them?

Jenni's stomach is flat, her feet sample-size—the same as my mother's—and her toes are all the right length.

She's had maybe three zits in her entire life.

What's the problem?

The problem is I spend a lot of time standing next to her. And standing next to Jenni makes me hideous.

I look Amazonian, and not like the Web site. Big, fat, hulking. Awkward, ungraceful, lumpish. I am average height, and like most American females, I hate my thighs.

My second toes are bigger than my thumb toes, and they're long and bony, where Jenni's are these perfectly formed little piggies.

My skin is oily and gets blotchy and Mom says I'll be thankful when I'm older, which only makes me pissed off at her—I hate it when people start sentences with things like, "When I was your age" or "If I only knew then."

Jenni will get these microscopic enlargements of her teeny tiny pores and look in the magnifying mirror and say, "Oh god, I'm disgusting."

If she wasn't so great, you'd want to kill her.

Or at least stab her with a mechanical pencil, or one of those cute corn-on-the-cob holders that looks like an ear of mini-corn, or something that wouldn't do a whole lot of damage but would make the point that she's perfect and if she thinks *she's* disgusting, what are you?

But you don't do anything because she's your best friend and you love her and everyone knows you as Alice-andJenni, which even sounds like it's supposed to go together, like the two of you unite to become a whole other person, maybe a girl named Alison Jenni, who is stronger and more confident than each is on her own, the result being more than summative, the new girl being somehow geometrically better than a simple joining of two addends.

Alice + Jenni = Girl Who Can Do Anything.

What Jenni doesn't have, what I bring to the mathematical equation, is academic ambition. It's not that Jenni isn't smart.

She is.

She just does things at a slower, more measured pace than me and wants everything to turn out perfect. Jenni is methodical. She makes patterns for her clothes; she follows directions when she bakes; she prints out instructions and looks at maps.

Often when we're doing homework at my house, Jenni will say, "I'm hungry. Do you want to eat something?"

And of course I always do, so we go downstairs and she looks through the fridge and takes out about eighty things, including three different kinds of mustard, mayo, a plastic container of lettuce, peanut butter, grape jelly, raspberry jam, smoked turkey, ham, tofu slices, gluten-free fake bacon slices, cheddar cheese in a block, presliced Colby, a nubbin of moldy Gouda, a cucumber, some parsley, and a sad tomato. Then she'll pull out a loaf of whole-wheat bread, and also a big round of sourdough, and some tortillas. She'll take two plates out of the cabinet, two knives, and when everything is spread all over the countertop she'll say, "Now. What do we feel like having?"

If my mom or dad happen to be around, she'll ask if she can make them a sandwich.

Mom never says yes, but she usually kisses Jenni on the head and says, "Thanks anyway, kiddo."

Dad almost always says, "Sure. Surprise me."

On my own, I'll just grab the bread that is closest, slather some peanut butter on it, plop on a dollop of jelly, wrap it in a paper towel, and go back upstairs.

Plates?

Why would you need a plate?

Then you'd have to put it in the dishwasher.

Jenni likes to know all her options, weigh them, and make a careful decision. When she constructs a sandwich, she will spread the mayo in smooth swipes so every inch of the bread is covered in a perfect, even layer. She will tear the lettuce into pieces that fit like puzzle parts. She'll fluff the ham and tofu slices so that there are air pockets and they don't lie flat.

She'll add salt and pepper, and, after she puts the other piece of bread on so all the dents in the crust line up, she'll cut it diagonally, and diagonally again into four perfect triangles. If she's making pb&j, she'll cut off the crusts. She leaves them on when the sandwich has meat.

She may or may not have a reason.

I've chosen not to ask.

I throw together combinations of peanut butter, Marsh-mallow Fluff, bananas, and potato chips. I'm a big fan of bacon and peanut butter sandwiches; sometimes I'll add some maple syrup and sometimes tomatoes. The craziest Jenni gets is mixing ham and tofu slices. Some of my creations get a little out of control and often I have a hard time stuffing the whole business into my mouth. Things fall out as I take a bite. Jenni, like Walter, nips politely at hers.

The funny thing is, when Jenni makes a sandwich for me, it always tastes better than anything I could have made for myself.

I'm not sure why this is, but she says the same thing about the sandwiches I make for her.

7

On the second morning of January, the tail end of the Year of the Dragon, after my first horrendous outing, I Googled "How to start running." I figured more information might help.

There were 1,330,000,000 results, and they all said basically the same thing: you walk for a while, run for a bit, walk, run, rinse, and repeat. That's kind of what I had ended up doing that first day, but not because I had some kind of plan.

I ran, ran out of steam, had to walk, got cold and ran to get warm, ran out of breath, and walked home.

So maybe it would be better if I tried to follow something more like a program.

I wrestled myself into the jeggings again and, when I caught a glimpse of my reflection in the mirror, thanked every deity I could name that the style had passed quickly. Then I pulled on the T-shirt and the sweatshirt, snuck Mom's sneaks from her shoe palace, and went out the door.

The experts and the non-expert-people-who-think-they're-experts on the Web said to warm up by walking fast for five to ten minutes.

They also said to make sure you had the right shoes. I wasn't about to ask Mom to buy me running shoes—it would make her too happy—so I decided to keep using hers, which she never wore anyway and so wouldn't notice they were no longer *pristine* ("remaining in a pure state").

After you warmed up, you were supposed to walk for something like six minutes, then jog for a minute, and then walk for six minutes, and then jog for a minute, and then walk for six minutes, and then jog for a minute, and then cool down.

Already I thought running was going to be really, really boring.

I was bored before I even started.

The jury seemed to be out on stretching. Some sites said to stretch, others said not to. They all seemed to agree if you were going to stretch, you should warm up for at least ten minutes before you attempt it. I'm not very stretchy—not like my mom and Jenni, who can bend over and kiss her knees while wrapping her arms around her straight legs or do a split anytime, anywhere—so I thought I'd listen to the experts and pretend-experts who said stretching was unnecessary.

I set out walking, faster than normal, and I swung my arms up and down, the way one of the Web sites had said. They would act as levers and propel me forward.

And guess what: they did.

The harder I swung my arms, the faster my legs moved.

I'm sure I looked like a windup toy soldier.

In the junk drawer in the kitchen I had found an old

sports watch, an ugly digital thing with a black plastic band. I hit the stopwatch and, after eight minutes, I started running.

Not fast.

They all said not to go too fast at the beginning.

My "run" was just a tad quicker than the arm-swinging walk. I did it for one minute, and then walked. After another six minutes, I was ready to run again.

This time I wanted to go faster.

Mistake.

Someone knifed me in the ribs. At least, that's the way it felt. Shooting pain in my right side nearly made me double over.

At forty-seven seconds I needed to stop.

But I didn't stop. I slowed down and was grateful for the walk time when it came, and eventually whatever demon had stabbed me went away.

The last run segment I took it easy.

When I was walking for the final interval, I felt like I could do another run. I decided to go for it.

I didn't hit the Start button on the watch this time; I just ran. I ran as hard and as fast as I could. I ran until my lungs pinched and my legs could barely leave the ground. I ran until I couldn't run another step.

In a weird way, it felt good to hurt, to feel as bad physically as I did inside. For a few moments, I was able to forget that I was a Yale reject.

8

Last spring Mom took me with her on an overnight trip to Columbus, Ohio, where she had a Continuing Medical Education conference. She made me come along so we could attend an Exploring College Options evening at some snooty private school called Thatcher Academy (how she found out about this event I have no idea), where admissions officers from Harvard, Duke, Georgetown, Stanford, and the University of Pennsylvania came and did presentations.

Here's what I learned: these colleges are exactly alike. They all had:

1. The smartest professors.
2. The prettiest campus.
3. The most spirited sports teams.
4. The most diverse student body.
5. The best food.
6. The greatest study-abroad programs.
7. The biggest libraries.
8. The richest and most successful alumni.

More than one presenter said you could take classes in fields you've never even heard of. When the Harvard chick mentioned "classical philology" she was right: I'd never heard of it.

So I looked it up on my iPhone while she was yammering.

Classical philology turns out to be the study of ancient Greek and Latin words.

The main differences, as far as I could tell, were among the people who gave the presentations. The lady from Duke, with shiny, precise hair, wore a trim navy-blue suit and pearls, smiled during her entire talk, and seemed genuinely thrilled to be there. I wondered if she was like Walter-the-Man's Deborah.

The dude from Georgetown, however, thought he was a stand-up comic and cracked jokes that were not at all funny. Often they were directed at the girl from Harvard, who looked younger than me and had to keep pushing up her glasses when she spoke.

During the slide show, she talked about how the university was founded in 1636 and named after John Harvard. She showed a photo of a statue of a man sitting in a chair. People in the audience began to whisper and giggle.

The Harvard girl turned to look at the slide and said, "Jason, you asshat!" and then covered her mouth with her hand while the guy from the University of Pennsylvania stood in the back of the room cackling. He'd jacked her PowerPoint presentation so the photo we saw was of Ben

Franklin, the founder of Penn, a much more recognizable figure than John Harvard, whoever he was.

These people had clearly been on the road together for too long.

Mostly parents asked the questions: "What's the acceptance rate?"

For Harvard and Stanford, it was single digits. They didn't need to spell out the math: only six students out of a hundred would get in. The percentages at the others were higher, but still, the odds were against you.

One girl raised her hand and wanted to know if it was better to take an honors class and get an A or take an AP and maybe get a B.

The comedian from Georgetown said, "Take the harder class and get an A!" The others nodded. People laughed not because it was funny but because everyone was so tense any opportunity to laugh was a gift.

"What's the median SAT score?" one dad wanted to know.

"Where do students get jobs after graduation?" asked a mom with puffy hair.

"What's the crime rate on campus?" a dad with a military bearing inquired.

"How many get into medical school?" There was no question in my mind that the dad who asked the question was a doctor.

These parents were starting to get on my nerves. It was like they were the ones going to college.

I looked at Mom in a way that said, *If you ask a question I will storm out of here and never speak to you again.*

According to Deborah via Walter-the-Man, the whole purpose of these nighttime programs was to generate more applications. Deborah described her job as getting the kids all excited about applying so she could deny them in the spring. The more applicants you deny, the fewer you accept, the more selective you look.

The last question of the night was about SAT prep classes. Were they worth the expense? The presenters all agreed that they could be helpful in boosting scores. When Mom heard that I could see her brain-wheels turning.

As we drove back to the hotel, she said she wanted to sign me up for a class. I said, "No way, José," something she said all the time.

"Why wouldn't you want to maximize your chances?"

I told her I'd study on my own.

"There might be tricks you could learn."

"I'm not a dancing elephant. I don't want to do tricks. I want to do it my way. By learning shit."

"Alice."

"What?"

"Can't you ever just be easy?"

9

After my second run, I had second thoughts about the wisdom of my New Year's resolution.

And third thoughts.

And 7,234th thoughts.

It was nearly impossible to get out of bed the next day. My legs felt like someone had put them through a meat grinder. My butt hurt, which was not surprising, but so did my arms, which was. If it wasn't already dead, my hair would have hurt.

But still, I stuffed myself into my jeggings and went out again the next day. And the next. And the next.

Pretty quickly I gave up on the idea of following a program. My running turned out to be a lot like how I make sandwiches. I can't ever seem to stop being me. Even though there are ways that I am superorganized, there are also ways in which I'm kind of a mess.

From all the stuff I'd read on the Web I learned the mistake most people make—the reason so many people hate running—is they start out too fast and then burn out and die. So instead of doing the whole timed walk-run thing, I forced myself to run slower than I thought I could.

Each day I ran for a few minutes longer than the previous time.

I tried to go when there weren't too many people around, but the boulevard was always swarming with runners. The worst was going past the playground, where I was afraid kids would point at me and laugh. They hadn't yet, but you can't trust kids not to laugh at you. Especially if you look funny, which I'm sure I did.

At one point, I tried this breathing technique I read about online where you inhale for three steps and exhale for two.

That did not go well.

I started to feel self-conscious about the way I was breathing. Then I spiraled into a bizarre analytical thought process where I decided my elbows were swinging weirdly.

My nose got all runny in the cold and of course I never brought any tissues with me. So I started using my sleeve to wipe it. Gross, I know.

Sometimes I'd have to walk. But one day about midway through switching between walking and jogging, I started to feel pretty good. I breathed easily and my legs didn't hurt and my feet didn't hurt and it didn't feel like my heart was going to burst. At one point, I was full-on sprinting and it was great. The sprinting probably only lasted, like, three seconds, but it felt like I covered a lot of ground fast.

I checked my watch and realized that I'd been running for just over thirty minutes. Thirty minutes of running!

I was so happy I ran for that long that I gave it a try again the next day.

Worst. Run. Ever. That run only lasted, like, ten minutes.

And that's the way it went. One good run, one (or two or three) bad ones. But the good ones felt so great, it kept me going.

Sometimes I'd get a song stuck in my head and hear it for the whole run. Usually I didn't know all the lyrics, so it would be the same lines over and over. Sometimes I noticed the leafless trees along the boulevard I'd never paid attention to before or counted the different colors of houses. I began to recognize people too, other runners. I'd see the older woman with the big poodle, the guy with the blaze-orange hat who went so fast I could hear him breathing as he zoomed by, the heavy man who ran even more slowly than me if you can believe it, wearing a UCLA sweatshirt and thick black sweatpants with long baggy shorts over them. He made me look like a *Project Runway* model.

Another time, I saw the tasty morsel with the Toto dog again. They ran really, really fast. And made me feel really, really slow.

10

It was one of those late-January after-school afternoons, gray and chilly, with a light dusting of snow on the ground, where all you want to do is curl up in a chair in a closet under a heavy blanket with a rat on your shoulder and read six novels. I contemplated going out for a run for about fifteen seconds, but:

1. Walter's cage needed cleaning.
2. I had to read "Shooting an Elephant" by George Orwell for English.
3. A 62.9-kg downhill skier was moving at a speed of 12.9 m/s as he started his descent from a level plateau at 123 m height to the ground below. The slope had an angle of 14.1 degrees and a coefficient of friction of 0.121. The skier coasted the entire descent without using his poles; upon reaching the bottom he continued to coast to a stop; the coefficient of friction along the level surface was 0.623. I had to figure out how far the dude would

coast along the level area at the bottom of the slope.

I opened the door to Walter's cage to see if the munch-kin wanted to come out. Since he'd been sleeping all day, he stretched one paw, reaching like Michelangelo's Adam trying to touch his finger to the finger of God on the ceiling of the Sistine Chapel. Then he flicked his wrist in the gay-positive gesture and made the biggest yawn you've ever seen. When you see something that adorable it kind of makes your heart hurt.

Walter's teeth are orangish yellow. They are big. Part of what it means to be a rodent is that your teeth never stop growing, so you have to do a lot of gnawing. For the *uninitiated* ("without special knowledge or experience"), his teeth can look kind of scary. Jenni freaked the first time she saw him yawn, but that's the only time you ever see his teeth. When he yawns. He never bites. He has never bitten anyone. Ever.

Walter is a clean freak. Not only is he an enthusiastic self-groomer, he also generously offers up his talents as a manicurist. After he's satisfied he's clean enough, he will come onto my lap and work on my nails. He thinks I'm *slovenly* ("messy or dirty"). He may be right. So I let him go about his business.

"It's good to have a job," I say to him. "Work, Walter, work."

While he keeps himself *pristine* (review: "remaining in

a pure state") and he always pees in the same spot in the corner of his cage, Walter's housekeeping skills leave something to be desired. I had to get him out of there so I could be his maid.

"Out, damned spot, out!" I said to him, quoting Lady Macbeth.

He ambled through the door of his cage and I picked him up and we smooched for a while. Then I put him on the floor and went to get a garbage bag. His cage is really easy to clean: there's a wire part that sits on top of a big plastic tray and I just dump all the litter into a bag, wash the bottom, and fill it up with fluffy fresh bedding. I did research when I first got him about what would be the best and safest environment for him.

Have I mentioned that I love doing research about rats?

Walter is a Norway rat, or *Rattus norvegicus,* also known as the brown rat. This is kind of funny since like many things having to do with rats, it's completely wrong. Norway rats are not from Norway and they are not necessarily brown. They are from Asia and they come in a Baskin-Robbins assortment of colors and hairstyles. There are rex rats that look like they have bad '80s perms and hairless rats that look like fetal pigs. There are also Dumbo rats, who are more round than pointy, with big circle ears set far back on their heads.

The American Fancy Rat and Mouse Association recognizes thirty-eight distinct colors, including champagne, chocolate, cocoa, lilac, mink, platinum, Russian blue, sky blue, cinnamon, cinnamon pearl, fawn, lynx, pearl, and blue point Siamese. Yes, you can have a Siamese rat.

The splotches on Walter's back make him, as far as I can tell, a *variegated* ("having patches, stripes, or marks of different colors") rat. I got him at the pet store in the mall before I did all my rat research and learned about breeders and ratteries.

When I brought him home that first day Dad began to recite a poem by Gerard Manley Hopkins called "Pied Beauty." *Pied* means "patchy in color, splotched, or piebald" and is a better word than *variegated*. I'm not sure I totally understand the poem but I love the way it sounds. It starts out: "Glory be to God for dappled things— / For skies of couple-colour as a brinded cow."

When I finished cleaning his cage, my own pied beauty was MIA. I looked around for him. Walter likes to snuggle in bed even when I'm not there. This requires an Olympian feat of scaling the quilt that hangs over the side. He gets a running start, launches himself so he lands a little way up, and then, hand over tiny hand, ascends. It's a bit like the rope climb we had to do in school: surprisingly hard. But Walter makes it look easy. You've never seen a more graceful, acrobatic rat.

When he arrives at the top, he does a crazy hop, kind of like a victory dance.

Walter wasn't on the bed.

He wasn't under the desk.

He wasn't back in his cage.

I called him.

Nothing.

Usually he comes running when I say his name. At times, I get scared I've lost him and walk around the room and yell, "Walter, Walter," and finally turn around to find he's been following me the whole time. The truth is, he's about as likely to run away from me as I am from him.

I looked over at the door to my bathroom and saw a long unbroken stream of toilet paper going from the bathroom, around the dresser, and continuing into the closet. I walked over to the closet, opened the door all the way, and there was Walter, concentrating so hard he didn't even hear me, busy making a fluffy bed of toilet paper in the corner.

I wondered about the coefficient of friction when it comes to dragging bathroom tissue.

I figured out that the skier would coast for 116 m (115.95, actually, but I rounded up) and then finished up the rest of my physics problem set, which was all about work and energy—balls being thrown, carts getting pushed, mugs of beer gliding along bar counters.

Ms. Chan had given me an extra-credit assignment for English. Even though I didn't need any more credit—I had the highest average in the class—we both pretended I did it for the grade and not because I was a dork who could never get enough homework. Ms. Chan asked me to write a report on George Orwell's essay "Shooting an Elephant." When she told me the title I was skeptical. I didn't want to read about dead animals.

"Trust me," she said.

"I thought you were never supposed to trust someone who said 'Trust me.' In fact, I thought you told us that."

She shrugged her shoulders and said, "It's your grade."

The essay totally rocked.

Orwell basically says *imperialism* ("extending the power of one nation over another one") is evil and then shows you how and why it's bad by telling a story. The story he tells made me cry. But when I'd gone through it a second time, I realized I'd cried at the wrong place. I cried when the elephant suffered and died but barely even noticed that a person had also been killed. And that's his point: imperialism dehumanizes the people in power as well as the colonized. After I finished my report, which got long because I wanted to look carefully at how he embeds his argument into what looks like a straight narrative, I settled in for a few rounds of Freerice.

Freerice is my favorite Web site.

You get a word.

You get four choices from which to pick the correct synonym.

If you're right, the program donates ten grains of rice to a developing country through the United Nations.

When you answer a bunch right, you go up a level.

You get smarter and you feed the hungry!

Free rice!

How much do I love this? I can't even begin to say. I've provided a lot of meals to starving people and have learned a ton of new words, which I like to share with Dad. He gets so happy on the rare occasions I find a word he doesn't know.

Jenni's nails had grown in. Though I missed the small bit of raggedness on her otherwise perfect person, I was happy her resolution had stuck. One afternoon when we were at a coffee shop we liked to go to called the Coffee Shop, I said, "Dudette—soon we'll be going for mani/pedis with my mom. Your nails look great."

She held up her cute paws and said, "Yeah, I've stopped biting them. Except for my left thumb."

And sure enough, the nail on her left thumb was chewed to the quick.

God, I love Jenni.

"It's like the intentional flaw in the Oriental carpet," I said.

"Huh?"

"You know—when they make carpets like the ones in my house with all the elaborate designs, the carpet makers always add a flaw because only Allah is perfect, and to try to create something perfect would be arrogant."

Jenni said, "How do you know this stuff?"

"Um, I'm perfect?"

Then she looked like she wanted to say something else, but didn't.

"What?"

"Nothing, really. It's just been hard lately. Kyle and I—"

I sighed really loud and said, "That old Kyle."

Whenever Jenni tries to talk about Kyle, I usually interrupt her by sighing really loud and saying, "That old Kyle."

And then Jenni tells me to shut my piehole.

And then I say, "Make me."

And then she rolls her eyes and shakes her head.

But this time, she didn't tell me to shut my piehole. She just raised a hand and looked into her latte.

Then she asked, "How's the running going?"

I had to stop to think.

"I didn't expect to like it so much. Sometimes it's hard to get out the door. When I don't feel like going, I can find a whole lot of other things to do, like alphabetize my books or clean my room or play Snood or Freerice. I put it off and put it off and then, finally, I remember it's my resolution and I need to at least stick to what I've said I'll do. So I pull on my jeggings and once I'm sausaged into them, I tell myself it will still count if I only go for ten minutes. Once I'm out, and I'm running, I start to feel good. It's like I have to trick myself into doing it, but when I do, I am happy to keep going."

Jenni gestured toward my half-eaten raspberry oat bar. I nodded, and she slid the plate to her side of the table.

"But here's the thing," I continued. "My shins are sore."
I pointed to the front of my legs. "Right here."

"Hmmm," Jenni said. "Probably a tendon issue, like shin splints. Might be an overuse injury. Some kind of inflammation." Because of Kyle, Jenni spoke sports. She also had a milk mustache and I pointed to my own upper lip. She got the message.

"What am I supposed to do about it?"

"I don't know. Probably you have to stop for a while. Red shirt. Be on the DL."

"Wear a red shirt? Be on the down low?"

"The disabled list."

"I don't want to stop," I said, surprised to hear this come out of my mouth.

"Why not ask your mom?"

"Right."

"Why not?"

"Because I don't want her to know I'm running."

"Why not? She said—"

"She said what?"

At this point, Jenni had finished her latte and looked over at mine, still half full. She raised her eyebrows. I nodded. She reached over and grabbed it. In that moment, she reminded me of Walter.

"Nothing. Never mind."

"If I tell her, she'll get all excited and will encourage me and I won't want to do it anymore."

"Al, she just wants to help. She thinks you spend too much time doing homework and need to develop—"

"I know. I know what she thinks. But it doesn't help me to have her breathing down my neck. It makes me not want to do anything."

"Alice," Jenni said, slurping the last gulp in the mug with a noise you would not have expected from a girl so pretty and petite, "sometimes you stand in your own way."

She was right. I *should* tell my mother. I needed to get better clothes and shoes that fit and she was going to have to buy them for me. The experts and nonexperts talked about technical fabrics that wick moisture from the body.

Wick? ("To absorb or drain.")

Each time I wore my T-shirt under my hoodie it would get soaking wet. It made sense there would be clothing designed especially for running.

Also, I know Mom is only trying to help. I feel bad about not being more grateful to her.

But the weight of her motherly love makes me cranky and I lash out.

I want to stop myself even as I am doing it.

I can't.

It's like something inside me takes over, a little alien, an evil little alien, who pops out periodically to make me say assholic things to people I care about.

I do this to everyone except Walter, who never does one single thing that annoys me. My mom gets the worst of the alien treatment.

That night, I waited until after dinner, when she had a glass of wine and was reading Martha Stewart's magazine.

"Mom," I said, "I have something to tell you but I don't want you to get all excited because if you do, it's going to ruin everything for me."

She set down her glass and the magazine and said, "When you put it like that, I can't wait to hear."

Dad looked up from doing a crossword puzzle on his iPad. When Mom and I start to get into it, he'll call out questions like, "What's a four-letter word for 'writes quickly'?" and since neither Mom nor I can resist being right we'll both shout out, "Jots," and sometimes we forget what we're arguing about.

My dad is sneaky like that.

"I've been running."

I waited.

Since she can't raise her eyebrows or furrow her brow, my mom generally has a pleasant expression on her face. If she's overdone it with the Tox, she can look surprised for three months.

I could see her eyes getting all shiny, and I knew she felt happy about what I'd said, so I needed to step in and cut her off.

"Don't say anything. Just let me talk."

She made the rolling motion with her hand that signaled for me to keep going.

"I've been borrowing your running shoes—"

She interrupted me. "Oh honey, you know my feet are smaller than yours. You need to have the right shoes, shoes that fit. You're going to get injured—"

"—and I need to get running shoes. And clothes. My shins already hurt—"

"You're at risk of developing tendinitis and—"

"Will you please listen to me? I'm doing something you said you wanted me to do, I'm getting exercise, okay, and now you're telling me how to do it? I was trying to ask you to buy me the right shoes and you wouldn't even listen to me. You never listen to me."

Dad said, "Don't you know someone who owns a running store, Sarah?"

Mom and I were locked in silent battle, each replaying previous skirmishes in our heads.

"We can go on Saturday," she said finally, and went back to reading Martha.

"Fine," I said.

"Fine," Mom said.

12

Sometimes my mother and I get along well. When Dad goes out of town on business trips, we have a tradition. Mom makes breakfast for dinner—the only meal she can cook—and we get a pound bag of peanut M&M's and watch chick flicks on Lifetime or old episodes of *Gilmore Girls*. Sometimes Jenni joins us, but often she has a game or is out with the stud muffin.

During these mostly cozy nights Mom will try to get me to talk to her.

She'll ask about school, and when I'm in a good mood, I'll tell her about a project I'm working on (a lab report on optics; a paper on *The Scarlet Letter*; reading the Federalist Papers) but when she tries too hard to get personal, when she asks me questions about boys, I get annoyed and say something bratty like, "Why can't you be more like Lorelai?"

She gets pissed and says, "Why can't you be more like Rory?"

In fact, I wish I was more like Rory. Jenni thought I was excited about Yale because that's where Rory Gilmore went.

But Jenni was wrong.

I don't make my life decisions based on TV shows.

Mom and I started fighting a whole lot more when she got obsessed with the college-admissions thing. She made me go with her on a big college tour at the end of the summer. I told her I didn't need to visit colleges; I only wanted to go to Yale and I didn't have to see it to be sure. I was going to apply early and that would be that.

She said I should keep my options open. She said I'd need to have backups in case Yale didn't work out.

I accused her of not having confidence in me.

In the end, I couldn't get out of the trip.

Some highlights:

1. Going to Yale we got ridiculously lost on the one-way streets in New Haven and ended up in some really sketchy parts of town. It was rainy and not quite as magical as I'd hoped. It was still my first and only choice.

2. At Trinity College a dad had a heart attack during the group information session and my mom was the closest thing around to a real doctor. So we waited with him for the EMTs and spent the afternoon with his daughter in the hospital.

3. When we stayed at the Four Seasons in Boston we got bitten by bedbugs, which was as uncomfortable as it was disgusting. All that money for an expensive hotel and it turns out

the beds were already occupied—with creepy critters.

4. Also in Boston, someone broke into our rental car and stole my laptop. I know, I shouldn't have left it in there, but I was tired because we'd been to Tufts, Boston University, and Harvard all in one day. Then I had to listen to Mom tell me eight thousand times that I shouldn't have left my computer in the car. Also in Boston, we had a blow-out fight (see above, under *computer loss*) and I told my mother I wanted to go to college, to any college, just so I could get away from her. She said, "Don't let the door hit you on the way out." I said, "Fine." She said, "Fine."

5. In Providence, Mom got food poisoning. She stayed in the hotel room and barfed while I did the tour of Brown. I felt guilty for being so happy to get away from her for a bit.

6. I managed to convince Mom to let us stop at the Ben&Jerry's factory on the way to see Middlebury. They had a "flavor graveyard," where headstones mark the deaths of flavors that didn't make it. It made me kind of sad to see where good ideas go to die.

7. Our rental car got a flat in western Massachusetts and while we waited two hours for AAA to show up, we had another giant fight.

8. A bunch of drunken frat boys at Amherst hung out the window of their house and screamed that Mom had a nice ass. I thought it was funny and laughed, and laughed even harder when she got mad at them, which made her mad at me too. I asked why she wore tight jeans and high heels if she didn't want people to notice her ass. Then she got madder at me and we didn't speak for the rest of the day.

9. The information sessions all sounded the same and were so boring I thought I was going to die. Except for the one at Trinity College, where the dad almost did die. Not funny.

10. I had on-campus interviews and Mom made me get dressed up, even though Walter-the-Man said Deborah said the interviews didn't matter. Most of them were awkward and painful. The guy at Wesleyan had a half-eaten PayDay on his desk and I told him I thought if Pluto could be fired from being a planet, PayDay should be banned from the candy aisle. We had a lively debate about what makes for a good candy bar, though he was completely wrong.

11. This was different from the interview with the woman at Dartmouth, who asked me with a straight face, "If you were a vegetable, what vegetable would you be?" I thought she was

kidding and laughed. She wasn't kidding. So I
thought about it for a minute and gave her an
answer I thought she was looking for. "I'd be
an artichoke," I said. "Why?" She leaned in, as
if she wanted to know. "Because I have a
prickly, tough exterior, but inside there's a big
warm and fuzzy heart."

Then she told me I was going to host a
dinner party and I had to invite twelve people
from any time in history. "Who would you
invite and where would they sit? Who would
be to your immediate right? Who would be at
the end of the table?"

When I get asked a question like this, my
mind goes blank. I couldn't think of one
person to invite to this made-up dinner party.
Finally, I said, "Ben Franklin." "Why?" she
asked. So I said, "He invented electricity. Well,
he didn't invent it, but he figured it out with
his kite-and-key experiment. He also invented
bifocal glasses and the Franklin stove—
which he didn't want to patent because he
thought people should be able to use his ideas
for free. He started the first fire station,
figured out how to predict storms, and
mapped the current of the Gulf Stream. He
invented the flexible urinary catheter when
his brother John suffered from kidney stones.

He was a postmaster, printer, and politician. He was a journalist, a businessman, a philanthropist, and a good swimmer. He invented swim fins! Swim fins! And the lightning rod! He calculated population growth! He invented a musical instrument called an armonica, which you played by rubbing the rims of glasses filled with water! And he wrote this funny letter to a horny young man on why older women make better mistresses. He was the Dr. Phil of the Founding Fathers."

Okay, so I got worked up, but how can you not love Ben Franklin? The Dartmouth lady looked weirded out and said, "That's one. Who else?" I told her Walter, and explained who he was. Let's just say it went downhill from there. She couldn't get comfortable with the idea of a pet rat. She cringed when I talked about him and that made me hate her.

12. Every night when we called home to talk to Dad and I asked him how Walter was doing, he'd say, "Fine." And I'd say, "What? Why did you say fine? Is something wrong?" And he'd say, "No, nothing's wrong. He's fine." "Then why didn't you say he's good?" "He's good, Alice." "Are you playing with him enough?" "Can I talk to your mother?"

At the end of the trip, I was more convinced than ever I wanted to go to Yale. I was a bit worried—though clearly not worried enough—about getting in. My test scores and grades were fine. But each of the colleges stressed the fact that their students had all done amazing, astonishing, unbelievable things before they turned eighteen. And the kids I met on the trip—you wouldn't believe how many familiar faces turned up on the campuses; we could have hired a bus and all traveled together—were quick to tell anyone who would listen just how amazing they were.

And if they didn't tell you, their parents did. You could see the parents sizing up the other kids and saying things like, "Oh, you're so lucky you don't come from New Jersey. There's practically affirmative action for people from less populous states." Or, "I heard it's much harder for girls to get in than for boys."

I think seeing these crazed, hypercompetitive parents was good for my mother. She backed off and said, "You'll end up at the right place for you, Al."

13

Saturday afternoon Mom and I went to the running store.

Even though I'd gone past it a zillion times, I'd never really noticed it. I could not believe there was a whole store devoted to running.

Are there also swimming stores?

And badminton stores?

As soon as we walked in the door, a tiny woman with a white-blond ponytail leaped up from a stool behind the counter and ran over to us. She said, "Dr. Davis! So great to see you!"

"Hello, Joan," Mom said, and hugged her. "This is my daughter, Alice."

The woman had a smile as big as the ocean and grabbed me by the shoulders to look at me, which struck me as quite odd since we were complete strangers.

She said, "Alice! I've heard so much about you. Still getting straight A's?"

I looked at Mom, trying to figure out who this person was, and when Mom gave me the look that said, *Don't ask because I can't tell you,* I knew the woman had been a patient. Doctors are not allowed to discuss their patients and my mom takes that seriously. Sometimes she'll slip up and mention talking to someone, like a news anchor or some local celebrity, and I'll say, "How do you know that person?" and she'll get quiet and say, "I can't say," and then I'll know exactly how she knows the person.

"How are you?" Mom asked, in a way that sounded too serious for the answer to be good.

"Good," Joan said. "Things are good."

Mom patted her arm and said she was glad to hear it. Then she told her we needed to get me outfitted with running gear.

"I didn't know you were a runner!" Joan said, her voice all bubbly again, as if she'd just found out I'd won a Nobel Prize. Her hair was pulled straight back from her face and when she turned to look at me, I could see she had lots of lines around her eyes, and freckles, so she clearly wasn't one of my mom's Botox chicks. She wore a stretchy long-sleeved shirt that fit so snug against her you could see the muscles in her stomach, a very muscular stomach. She sported loose yoga-y pants. The woman didn't have a butter pat's worth of fat on her. As hard as her body was, her voice was soft and girlish.

"I'm not a runner," I said. "I'm trying. Just started."

"If you're running, you're a runner!" she said. "Now, let's have a look at your feet."

Joan made me take off my shoes and socks and spent a long time examining my bare feet, which made me uncomfortable because my feet are ugly.

I mean, everyone's feet are ugly—except for Jenni's—but mine are the worst.

She watched me walk, made me stand, and finally sent me out the door to run down the block in a variety of shoes.

I couldn't tell much difference between them, but Joan said I was a "slight overpronator," which seemed like it could be insulting. She explained that most people either pronated or supinated, and that this had to do with how your foot rolled in or out after you landed.

The shoes she picked for me were hideous: yellow slabs, with pink and blue stripes, two down, two across. I didn't mind so much that they were unattractive, but they made my feet look gigantic. There was a nicer, more streamlined purple pair with gray highlights I liked better, but Joan said those weren't right for me.

And besides, she said, real runners don't care what their shoes look like.

Mom said it was important I not get injured, and it wasn't a fashion show.

I pointed out that was easy for her to say, in her Italian leather boots. She rolled her eyes.

My mother and Joan stood in front of the store and watched me while I ran down the street in different shoes. The best pair felt a whole lot springier than the ones I'd been wearing. I felt like I ran faster than I ever had and that I could keep going for a long time.

Joan said, "Whoa, there, doggie! Come on back." She

asked if that was my normal pace, and I got embarrassed. "It's okay," she said. "It's good to be excited about running. I am!"

I knew this.

I could hear it in her voice and see it on her face. Everything about her said she loved running and loved to talk about it.

We found me a pair of black tights, a long-sleeved shirt with a zipper, a vest that blocked the wind, and some socks. "Never, ever wear cotton socks," Joan said, "unless you want to end up with blisters. Believe me, I know a thing or two about blisters."

She measured my chest, which would have been embarrassing except Joan was easy to be around and nothing seemed like a big deal to her, and fitted me for a sports bra for which I practically had to do yoga to get over my shoulders.

The back wall of the store was entirely covered with square pieces of paper with numbers on them. Some had names, and some had writing. The word START was painted below the ceiling in big black block letters.

"What are all those numbers on the wall?" I asked.

She smiled. "Ah," she said. And instead of answering, she went over to a rack of brochures and flyers, pulled one out, and handed it to me.

"Are you busy a week from tomorrow?"

I was never busy on Sundays.

I shook my head.

"Can you get up early?"

"If I have to," I said. For a teenager, I was an early riser. Jenni didn't make it out of bed before noon on the weekends, and so I could never count on her to do anything before midday.

"I'm putting on a race—a 10K." She must have seen that I was confused and said, "That's 6.2 miles. One of my volunteers just bailed and I need someone to be on the course to help direct runners." She reached under the counter and pulled a red shirt out of a box with tons of red shirts just like it. It said *Red Dress Run* on it and had a drawing of a bunch of men and women running, all wearing red dresses. She waved it in front of me and explained that many runners would be wearing red dresses.

"Why?" I asked.

"Because it's fun and funny. And it's Valentine's Day," Joan said, as if it was the most obvious thing in the world.

I said, "Oh."

"Would you be willing to work for a shirt?"

"Do I have to wear a dress?"

"Not unless you want to."

I thought about it for a minute and said yes, I would. Volunteer. Not wear a red dress.

Joan rang up our purchases and the total amount was a very high number.

Mom handed me the bag and said what she always says when she buys me something: "Wear it well." That's what her mother used to say to her. I never met my grandmother— she died before I was born—but my mother talks about her, especially when shopping. Shopping was one of the things they loved to do together.

Joan said she looked forward to seeing me at the race, and I said it sounded like fun, which maybe it would be.

Mom thanked her and smiled at me in a way that made me tell her she had lipstick on her teeth even though she didn't.

14

The next day I put on my new clothes and, get this: I felt different, like I was a real runner. When I headed out the door I ran stronger and faster than ever. My new shoes might have had wings attached to them, like the sandals that belong to the god the Greeks called Hermes and the Romans renamed Mercury.

I made it to the boulevard and could not believe how easy it was. I zoomed along and passed people right and left, all forward motion. I thought about what I'd learned in physics and how I had not only speed, the equation for which is distance divided by time, but also velocity, which is change in position over time.

I was a vector; I had magnitude and direction.

Then it all fell apart.

Somehow I had managed to run into what Jenni calls the Drop Zone or the DZ. She'll come over, won't say a word to me except, "I'm in the DZ," and head straight to the bathroom. I don't know where she came up with Drop Zone, except it probably has something to do with spending so much time with jocks. There's also the PZ, the Pee Zone. They work the same way. I'm sure I don't have to explain.

Every step I took made the feeling in my gut worse. I had to stop, walk, and waddle home. I thought I might not make it in time. That I did well in physics and understood Newton's three laws of motion didn't change the fact I barely made it to the downstairs bathroom. I'd never felt so relieved—or so much like a loser.

I could hardly control my own bowels, much less my destiny.

Walter-the-Man was parked in front of the TV in the Walter-the-Man-shaped dent in the couch watching a Duke basketball game. My parents were nowhere to be found.

"Yo," he said.

"Hey," I said, and came in and sat beside him.

He screamed, "GET IT TOGETHER! Did you see that? That was a foul. Are these refs blind? THAT WAS A FOUL, YOU DICKWEEDS!"

When he watched basketball games, Walter-the-Man tended to scream a lot. I used to find it amusing.

"Help a fellow out? Fetch a fellow a beer?"

Instead of arguing like I normally do, I went into the kitchen and got one for him. He held out his hand for the bottle.

"Still sulking, I see."

"I'm not sulking."

"NOT ANOTHER THREE! COME ON, GUYS, STOP TRYING FOR THE THREES."

And then, "Looks like sulking to me."

"I suck," I said.

"And why is that?"

"You know why."

"Tell me." He screamed, "YES, OH YES! YES!!" and put his hands together as if he was praying, and clapped them like a lunatic as the ball went through the net.

"Vaseline! VASELINE!"

Maybe he said, "Gasoline." Or maybe "Maybelline." I had no idea what he was saying because he wasn't talking to me anymore. He cheered for the team as if he was the sixth man, as if they could hear him, as if his coaching advice—"OUTSIDE! GOOD GOLLY, MISS MOLLY! WATCH THE OUTSIDE MAN!"—was going to be heeded by these five guys on the court miles away and visible only on TV.

He looked hard at me and said, "Okay, Alice, tell me why you wanted to go to Yale."

"Why are you doing this?"

"Doing what?"

"You know all I ever wanted was to go to Yale."

"And now?"

"Now my life is pretty much over."

He thought about it for a minute, rubbed his head with his hand as if he was shining his scalp, looked back at the TV, and said, "ARE YOU KIDDING ME? ARE YOU GODDAMN FREAKING KIDDING ME?"

I slumped down farther in the couch and after two more baskets, Walter-the-Man started in again. "You're probably right. If you don't go to Yale, you are never going to amount to anything. I'll make you an offer. How about if I give you seed money and you can start a meth lab—put all those math and science skills you worked so hard to acquire to use."

"It's not funny."

"No, it's not. You're driving your mother crazy. She's worried about you. Everyone's worried about you. Plus, you're messing with my ability to enjoy watching young people chase each other around the court. So tell me, why did you want so badly to go to Yale?"

"Are you kidding?"

"No, Alice, for once I'm not. Tell me."

I let out a big sigh. And then I had to wait for another outburst to end.

Walter-the-Man said, *"Good look."*

Walter-the-Man said, "REBOUND! REBOUND! YES, HE GETS FOULED. ANOTHER SHOT. TAKE YOUR TIME, TAKE YOUR TIME. YES! YES! YES!"

Walter-the-Man said, "Tell me. Why Yale?"

"Because—I mean, it's obvious. It's one of the top schools in the world—the third oldest in North America after Harvard and William & Mary. Three of the nine Supreme Court justices are Yalies. Take a look at the biographies of the poets in *The Norton Anthology*. Tons of them went to Yale. They have secret societies, like Skull and Bones and Scroll and Key. The Frisbee was invented when Yale students tossed pie tins at each other, and pizza and hamburgers both originated in New Haven."

Walter-the-Man watched me as I talked. He no longer seemed interested in the game.

So I continued, "Yale has a copy of the Gutenberg

Bible—it's in the Beinecke Rare Book and Manuscript Library, which is made of translucent marble. A building with no windows but whose walls let light come in. The Payne Whitney gymnasium is known as the Cathedral of Sweat. The Yale Center for British Art has the most comprehensive collection of British Art outside the United Kingdom, housed in a building designed by the architect Louis I. Kahn, who also designed the Yale University Art Gallery, which also has an impressive collection. In one of the freshman dorms there's a room reserved for any Vanderbilt descendant who attends. The last one was Anderson Cooper. Yes, that Anderson Cooper, class of 1989. Jodie Foster, Meryl Streep, Paul Newman, Hillary Clinton (and her husband) are also alumni. Cole Porter wrote the fight song, 'Bulldog.'" I was winded by the time I finished.

Walter-the-Man said, "I see."

He shined his head again and sat up straight and said, "SONS OF COUSINS OF DAUGHTERS OF BITCHES! Guard your man, you pencil-necked geek. YES! YES! DENIED! DEEEEE-NIED!"

He looked at me and said, "You sound like you should be walking backward. Now, tell me, future tour guide: What does any of that have to do with why you want to go there? Do you aspire to be a poet or a Supreme Court justice? Are you a Vanderbilt? I suspect you're not going to go to be a frequenter of the gym, nor did I know you were interested in art, British or otherwise. Sure, you like pizza, but guess what? You can get it anywhere."

"And your point is?"

"My point is you've collected a lot of facts and still haven't given me one reason why Yale would be a better place for you than any of the hundreds of other schools you could attend."

"Ms. Chan went there," I said in a small voice.

True, my English teacher had gone to Yale. But she'd also said she'd never used the words *Yale* and *happy* in the same sentence. It was a pressure cooker; she said she thought she would have been happier someplace else. I didn't feel the need to share this fact with Walter-the-Man.

"Why Yale, Alice?"

"Because I've wanted to go there for forever. Because it was my dream."

"So dream a different dream."

Then he hit himself on the forehead and said, "Christ on a crutch, I sound like a goddamn greeting card."

He got serious again. He had the lines between his eyes—the elevens—that my mother eradicated with Botox from the foreheads of women who never wanted to frown.

"You know what I think?"

"I bet you're going to tell me. I bet I couldn't do anything to stop you from telling me." I let out another big sigh.

"Right you are. I get that you're upset. But I don't think it's because you wanted to go to Yale so badly. I think it's because, for the first time, you didn't get what you wanted. Or what you thought you wanted."

I could feel my mouth start to quiver and I bit down on my lip.

"It's not that," I said, though even as I said it I realized it *was* partly that.

I thought about how wounded Mom had looked when I told her about the REJECT notice and how shocked Jenni had been, and how I worried Jenni wouldn't think I was smart anymore. I'd always been the smart one.

"Maybe you're right," I said, my voice rough and crackly. "Maybe it was just the idea of Yale I wanted. But I told everyone about it and I assumed I was going to get in and now they think I'm a loser."

Walter-the-Man spent a while looking at his beer and then took a long sip. He said, "I went to a crappy state university and a crappy law school. Am I a loser?"

I shook my head because I no longer trusted myself to speak.

"Alice, there are many measures of success. One of the biggest failures is not to aim high enough. Google 'Teddy Roosevelt' and 'the arena'—you'll see. Me, too often I've settled for the easy stuff. I've managed to cruise through life without ever stretching, without ever really testing myself. I look at you and I think, you're going to *do* something. Okay, you didn't get into Yale. So what? Neither will most of the other kids who applied. Big freaking deal. You tried. You'll go on. You'll *do* something."

He took a final swig of his beer and continued. "You've had time to sulk and feel sorry for yourself, but enough, okay? No one died. No one got hurt. No one lost a limb or a job or a marriage. You will go to college. You will likely go to a fine college. You'll be fine."

He rubbed his hand over his head yet again and then dragged it across his face.

"I know what you're running away from, Alice," he said, and motioned toward my shoes. "It's the notion that you failed. You're running away from your own shame. What are you running toward? Can you figure that out?"

He shook his empty beer bottle at me. "And now, would you please go get me another beer? And, Alice? Get one for yourself. You need to chill the hell out."

PART TWO

Even though I usually got up early for a teenager, I was still a teenager. Six o'clock in the morning seemed like a ridiculous time to be awake.

Walter had only a little out-of-cage time, while I put on my running clothes, before I headed for the door. I thought it would be a good idea to wear stuff that would make me look like I fit in, even if I wasn't a real runner. Because it was also cold, I layered on a bunch more stuff—including my father's old Bowdoin sweatshirt. I hadn't washed my hair so I jammed it under a fleece hat that Jenni had made for me. She said she didn't want to knit me a wool cap because if I got sweaty, I'd smell like a wet dog.

It's a good thing Mom's car had GPS. The race was way out in the boonies and the directions listed a bunch of unfamiliar roads.

When I finally got to Country Homes Lane, Gladys, the lady in the GPS, said, "Turn right on James Road in one mile."

Okay.

Then she said, "In half a mile, right turn."

I wanted to say, *I heard you the first time. I can remember for half a mile.*

Then she said, "In one-tenth of a mile, right turn."

"Shut up, Gladys."

Then she said, "Right turn. Right turn." And went *ding.*

I was so busy being mad at her I drove past James Road.

I could practically hear her thinking, *Why can't this loser follow simple directions?*

All she said was, "Recalculating." But I felt it was in a snide tone.

In my family we call her Gladys, this domineering though often helpful voice. It's because Gladys is the patron saint of parking spaces. Whenever we drive downtown and need to find a place to park, we have to say the prayer. It might be strange for secular Jews like us to say a prayer, let alone believe in a patron saint of parking, but I'm telling you, it works. It goes like this:

Gladys, Gladys, full of grace
Help us find a parking space.

When you find one—which you always will if you pray to Gladys—you have to say, "Thank you, Gladys," or she won't help you again.

So after she told me to turn around and turn left (*"Turn left,"* she said, and I swear her bossy voice got louder), I made the turn and eventually found my way to the New

Hope fire station. The directions said we were supposed to park along the side of the road, and I did, thankful I didn't have to invoke the Gladys prayer because, frankly, I was done with her.

People dressed in the red shirt Joan had showed me in the store scurried around setting up folding tables. A big digital clock ticked off numbers. All of a sudden I felt nervous. What was I doing here?

What a stupid, stupid idea.

As soon as I got out of the car, I heard my name. Joan had spotted me and she came running over.

"Alice!" she said. "I'm so glad you made it."

I didn't know what to say, so I said, "Um. Thanks."

"I decided I want to have a water station at the turn and I'll need you to help man—I mean, person—it. I have all the stuff in the car and I'll drive you out. Miles should already be there and he can show you what to do."

She gave me a twinkly look and said, "You'll like Miles."

We got into her car, crammed with orange traffic cones, a folding table, stacks of paper cups, jugs of water, a box of red shirts, and four pairs of dirty running shoes. She said, "We'll drive along the course so you'll see what it's like for the runners. Someday you may want to get yourself a red dress and run this race."

There were orange cones along the shoulder. No sidewalks out here in the boonies.

"We can't close the roads, so runners have to be careful. You know to run on the side of the road facing traffic, right?"

No, I didn't. I thought you were supposed to be like a bike, going with the flow.

"Um, sure," I said.

"There's the mile mark," she said, and I saw a white line about two feet long painted on the road. "Every mile is marked like that. We don't have enough volunteers to call out splits, but so many people run with Garmins now it's not a big deal."

I had no idea what she had just said.

"What do you mean by 'splits'?" I asked. If people had to stop and do a split while running, this sport wasn't for me.

"Oh!" she said. "I forgot you're a newbie! Splits are the time at each mile. If you don't have a Garmin, a watch with a GPS system"—she held up her tiny wrist to show me the biggest and ugliest watch ever made, way bigger and uglier than the black plastic one I'd snagged from the junk drawer—"and if you don't have a good sense of pace, it's useful to know how fast you've run a mile. You want to start out at a pace you think you can hold, and, if possible, run the second half the same pace or even faster. If you run the second half faster than the first half, it's called a negative split."

She patted my leg. "Don't worry. You'll learn our language. And you'll find out about all the things only runners know."

We got to a dead end and Joan stopped the car.

She said, "The course turns onto the trail here. It's only two miles back to the start. You'll work the water station and direct runners onto the course." She took out the folding table, the water, and the cups, and plopped them on the side of the road.

She said, "Miles should be here any minute."

Right then, out of the woods, popped a guy in running tights carrying a backpack.

The cute guy from the boulevard. This time, he didn't have the Toto dog.

2

"Miles! Meet Alice! You two are working the water station! Thanks!"

Like a pocket pet, Joan moved in quick bursts. She slipped back into her car and drove away.

"Um," I said.

"Hey," he said, and raised a hand. "I'm Miles." He was even cuter when he wasn't running away from me.

I didn't know what to say, so I said, "Miles."

"I know, I know," he said. "I've heard all the jokes. Miles the distance runner. It's a family name, okay?" He smiled and then he looked down at the ground.

I hadn't even made the connection. I had never met anyone named Miles.

"So let's get set up," he said, unfolding the table. "Nothing worse than runners who don't have their water when they want it."

He grabbed the gallon jugs, ripped off the lids, tore open the plastic bag with the paper cups, and began to fill them. He moved quickly and his hands were shaking a little. I stood and watched.

"So, Alice, right? Want to pitch in?"

"Oh," I said. I didn't know what to do with myself and wished I had washed my hair. "Sure. Yeah."

I picked up one of the water bottles, which was heavier than I expected, and filled a cup.

"Yikes!" Miles said, and made the *enough* motion with his hands. "You only need to fill them halfway." But when he moved his hands, he knocked over a whole row of cups.

I laughed. He smiled and shrugged his shoulders. He had the best smile I'd ever seen.

"You race?" he said.

"I don't even really run. I mean, I just started. I have no idea what I'm doing here."

"Well, I'm confident you'll be able to handle the challenge of working a water station. All we have to do is make sure there are plenty of cups on the table—half full—and point the runners toward the trail." He gestured into the woods. On the ground was a giant white arrow that could have been made out of baby powder.

"What's that stuff?" I asked.

"Flour," he said. "It's how we mark the course. It's a pretty obvious turn, but still. I did the last two miles on my way here."

We continued to fill the cups and lined them up near the edge of the table.

He looked at his watch, not quite as big as Joan's, but still substantial, and said, "Plenty of time before the lead pack comes through. Might as well get comfortable." And he sank down on the ground and rested against a tree.

He dug into his backpack and pulled out a puffy jacket,

which he put on. I saw the outline of a book and wondered what it was. He riffled through the pack and offered me food: "Orange? Banana? Inedible energy bar?"

"Um, no thanks."

His legs were doing that boy thing, twitching as if they were being electrocuted. I didn't know what to do with my hands, so I pulled them inside my sleeves and rolled the bottom of the sweatshirt around my arms. Then I thought about what a dork I must look like and shook them out.

"I think I've seen you running," I said finally.

He looked at me, raised his eyebrows. His eyelashes were so long and thick they would have made Jenni jealous.

"On the boulevard," I said.

He nodded.

"With a dog. With a little *Wizard of Oz* dog."

"Potato," he said. "The Tater Tot. I take him with me when I run in town. Harriet—my grandmother—complains that all he does is lie around and eat bonbons and watch *Animal Planet,* so I try to take him a few times a week and he loves it and it keeps him from porking out too much. Harriet says animals should have a waist, even terriers." He'd said it all without taking a breath.

"Why do you call her Harriet?"

"That's her name?" He said it like a question.

"I mean—" He made me so nervous.

"Kidding. I know what you mean. Harriet's a kick. Truth is, most of the time I call her Harry. She's a photographer and has lived all over the world and she says she isn't old enough to be a grandmother."

"How old is she?" I asked, and realized what an idiotic question that was. I made half circles in the dirt with my foot. I was afraid if I looked at him some kind of gravitational collapse would take place in my body and I'd turn into a black hole.

He laughed and said, "Believe me, she's old enough to be a grandmother, just in a bit of denial. She walks with Potato every day, eats only organic food, and can twist herself into a pretzel. She'll probably outlive us all."

He patted the ground next to him. "Take a load off." He seemed to be relaxing but he still talked fast.

I looked down at my thighs in my tights and wondered if he'd said "load" because he thought I was a chunk. I also wondered if he noticed how bowlegged I was. I didn't want him to see how my knees could not come together and so I sat.

"You go to the high school?"

"Yeah," I said. "Senior." And I thought, oh no, let's not have the college talk. I couldn't bear to tell this guy about my sorry situation. "You?"

"Junior."

"Haven't seen you around school."

"Homeschooled."

He must have seen something on my face because he added, "Don't worry. We live off the grid, but not in any survivalist, antigovernment, Bible-thumping way. My parents are hippie-artist types and thought they could do a better job of teaching me than what I'd get in the public school system. Mostly I teach myself."

Then he bounced to his feet and said, "Here they come," and I thought maybe he meant his parents.

He clapped his hands. A small, wiry guy with cropped dark hair in a short, tight, stretchy red dress came running down the road.

"Great job, Nate," Miles said. "Looking good."

"Miles," the guy said, breathing out hard. "Need you here to pull me." He whooshed past the table and made the turn into the woods. He was out of sight when he called, "Congrats on yesterday."

Miles yelled, "Thanks!"

I thought: here we are in the boonies to provide water for runners and the dude didn't even take any. What's up with that?

I said:

1. "How come he didn't take any water and
2. what did he mean by needing you to pull him and
3. what happened yesterday?"

I got so caught up in the moment I forgot to be nervous and sounded like myself for the first time that morning.

Miles said, "The fastest runners won't stop for water in a race this short."

I thought, if six miles is short, what's long?

He continued. "And, well, he meant I'm usually ahead

of him." He adjusted the cups so they were in perfectly even rows. "When you're running behind someone, it can feel like you are being pulled along by them."

"You mean if you were running, you'd be in first place?"

No other runners were in sight. That guy Nate was far ahead of the rest of them.

"Yeah, probably."

"So what happened yesterday?" I asked again.

"Won a race."

"How long was it?"

"A half."

He looked uncomfortable.

"A half what?"

"Half marathon."

"You won a half marathon yesterday?"

He nodded and said, "Small race. None of the fast guys showed up."

"Um, how far is that?"

"13.1"

"Miles."

"What?"

"No. 13.1 miles?"

"Yes."

"Wow," I said.

3

Miles and I spent more than two hours together at the water station. It felt like fifteen minutes. Not only was it a blast to hang out with such a hot guy, it was a hoot seeing all these people, men and women, running through the woods wearing red dresses. Some had straps, some had long sleeves, some were polyester ruffled prom gowns, and some were similar to things I'd seen in my mother's closet. Many of the men also had on red lipstick and a few wore wigs.

According to Miles, runners would go to thrift stores looking for the "best" dress. As soon as he said that I wondered if I would see one of them wearing something that had come from my house.

A supertall guy in a poufy low-cut gown had two giant balloons to fill out the bust. Right as he got to our table, he swung his arm to reach for a cup of water and one of his "boobs" popped.

Miles laughed so hard there were tears in his eyes.

Many of the women wore red dresses too, but they seemed less giddy about the whole thing. Others wore what seemed to be skirts made for running. I couldn't wait to tell Jenni about those.

After the fastest people passed by without stopping for a drink, the slower ones grabbed our carefully placed cups. Miles clapped and cheered and encouraged them all. Many of them, especially those at the front of the pack, knew him and barked out congratulations. One guy in a sparkly spaghetti-strap number that would have made Nina Garcia sneer stopped, guzzled four cups of water, and asked Miles a bunch of questions about the half marathon. Miles just said, "I had a good day," and tried to shoo the guy along by saying, "It's a race, Dean, get going." When he ran off I could see that he had slit his dress up the sides so he could move his legs. Tim Gunn would have approved, even if Nina sneered.

When the runners came in big groups, we had to hustle to make sure all the water cups were filled. I understood why we only poured half a cup the first time I saw a guy pick one up, pinch it, and funnel the water into his mouth. The people who didn't pinch tended to spill a bunch down the front of their shirts, or to cough it out. The fastest runners grabbed, pinched, poured, and threw the empties on the ground. I must have looked surprised because Miles told me this was not rude; we had a big plastic garbage bag and we needed to collect the trash. "We're here to support the runners," he said.

But some of them looked for the bag anyway, and most of them thanked us for being out there. I could not believe how nice they were. Miles kept up a mostly supportive commentary as they ran past:

"Owen—how can you be so fast when you run so funny?" It was true—the guy's legs kicked out behind him and off to the sides. The guy gave him a big smile and flipped him the bird.

"Jonathan, way to go!"

"Nice job, Candace—looking strong! Guess that Cross-Fit training is paying off!"

"Kevin—isn't this race too short for you? It's only a 10K, not a hundred."

"David, always smooth."

"Ruth, you have movie-star legs!"

After a while, things spread out and long minutes passed between people. As I watched the parade of runners, I was surprised by how many shapes and sizes they came in. I saw there is no such thing as a "runner's body." Some looked smooth and efficient, and others—even those who were in the front—did not seem like they should be able to move so fast.

Miles and Joan, both skinny, compact, and typically athletic, were, I realized, kind of exceptional. Plenty of people at the race had extra pounds around their middles, or substantial boobs and womanly hips, and some of the men had big bellies and some even had what you'd have to call blubber butts. Or no butts at all.

They also spanned the ages. The youngest was an eleven-year-old girl who ran superfast, and the oldest was, no kidding, old. I mean, great-grandfather old. But when he came through our water station he was far from last. He had on a baseball cap with a feather sticking out of it and he greeted Miles with a slap on the shoulder and a smile that made it look like there was nowhere on earth he'd rather be, and nothing he'd rather be doing. He up-ended a cup of water into his mouth, said, "Gotta go," and booked down the trail.

"That's Bob Hayes," Miles said, after the man had made the turn. He said it the way you might say "That's Bill Gates" or "That's Scarlett Johansson." Or even, "That's God."

"Eighty-six and still doing marathons."

I did the math in my head. "26 miles?" I'm sure Miles thought I was brilliant.

"26.2."

Toward the end, small groups of mostly women jogged or walked, laughing and talking. As they came by they said things like, "What a great day for a run," and a tall woman with long blond hair looked at me and asked, "Aren't we fortunate to be able to be out here doing this?" She thanked me for giving up my Sunday morning to help.

When I said to Miles that the people at the back of the pack seemed to be having more fun than the fast ones, he said, "It's a different kind of fun. Personally, I can't imag-ine doing a race and not going as hard as you can, but whatever."

After the last runners had come through, Joan drove

up in her car and we loaded in the table and the now-full garbage bag, and she thanked us in her perky voice and drove off.

Stunned that she would leave us in the middle of nowhere, I looked at Miles and said, "WTF?" Then I got embarrassed because what if he didn't like girls who curse, even though, technically, I had not cursed.

"Now we sweep the course," he said.

I thought: Sweep? Are you kidding me? We have to clean up all that flour he spilled on the ground?

Miles had crammed all his stuff into his pack and slung it on his back. Then he raised his chin toward the trail.

"Wanna?" he asked.

"Wanna what?"

"Run. Go ahead, take the lead. We'll just do the last part of the trail to make sure no one has gotten hurt or lost."

He said it would be slow, since he'd raced the day before and had done a shake-out run that morning. "We've got just two miles back to the start," he said, and I thought, right. Just two miles.

I began running, and was winded in about four steps. I could barely hear Miles behind me—he ran silently and didn't seem to need to breathe.

Miles must have heard me panting. People on the other side of the ocean probably heard me panting.

"So what do you like to read?" he asked.

"Books," I barked out. I could not manage more than one syllable at a time.

"Here, let me go ahead," he said, and he glided past,

brushing me on the arm as he went by. Then he slowed way down. He said, "Do you know why a marathon is 26.2 miles?"

Even though the pace had slackened, and my view had improved—his butt in those tights was supercute—I still couldn't catch my breath. No way could I have a normal conversation while running. Miles seemed to sense this. He just started talking.

"So, the legend goes that the distance is 26 miles to commemorate the run of Pheidippides, a messenger sent from the ancient battlefield of Marathon to the city of Athens to announce that the Athenians had defeated the Persians. He ran the whole 26 miles, burst into the assembly, blurted out, 'We won!,' and dropped dead. The extra 0.2 miles was added in the 1908 Olympics so the race could end in the stadium in front of the royal family."

"Huh," I managed to snort.

"Now that account is pretty bogus. Herodotus—you know, the Greek historian?"

I made a noise that I hoped came out as *uh-uh* but probably sounded more like a grunting pig.

"Well, Herodotus mentions a messenger named Pheidippides who ran from Athens to Sparta asking for help and then ran back—it was about 150 miles each way. No mention of him dropping dead. That would make him the father of the ultramarathon as well. Do you know about ultras?"

(Pig noise from me again.)

"So an ultra is any race longer than the 26.2 miles of the marathon."

"Longer?"

"Yeah. Next step up is usually 50K—31 miles. Then there are 50-milers, 100Ks, and 100-milers."

He went on to tell me about all these crazy-long races that took place in the woods, where people ran through the middle of the night. They had water stations like ours, Miles said, that provided a buffet of snacks: cookies, chips, M&M's, Gatorade, boiled potatoes, chicken noodle soup, pb&j sandwiches. Runners stopped, grabbed a handful of calories, and kept running. Miles had volunteered at some of them and that's where he'd first met eighty-six-year-old Bob Hayes. That guy didn't start running until he was sixty, Miles said, and now he's done a bunch of 50- and 100-mile races, and it didn't look like he was ever going to stop. Miles said that you get these giant silver rodeo belt buckles for finishing 100-mile races in under twenty-four hours. I don't know what seemed stranger: running 100 miles in one day or a skinny runner dude wearing a big metal belt buckle.

Miles talked and talked like a teacher lecturing about a subject he really loves. I listened and occasionally made the sound of a barnyard animal. I couldn't believe it when we passed through a clearing and I could see the fire station where the race started. We were back already. Miles had talked the whole way and I'd been concentrating so hard on what he was saying that I had forgotten to be freaked out about running with him.

While it wasn't easy, it was by far the best two miles I had ever run.

4

We arrived as they were giving out the prizes for sixty-to-sixty-four-year-old women. Joan announced the names, and she gave each person, no matter whether they had earned first, second, or third place, a chocolate heart and a big hug.

The man who won the race came over to talk to Miles. He still wore his tight red dress and I have to say, he had a better body for it than many of the *Project Runway* models. He carried a gigantic chocolate bar, which I assumed was his reward for winning.

I wondered, briefly, whether, if Miles had entered the race and had won the bar, he would have tried to share it with me, the way he'd offered me a piece of every item he'd pulled out of his backpack. Maybe he would have even given it to me, like a boyfriend would win a stuffed animal at the state fair for his girl. I'd carry it around and everyone would know that—

I had to mentally slap myself upside the head.

A bunch of other guys came around to ask Miles about his half marathon the day before. They were speaking running. I edged away.

People were busy taking down the finish line and when Joan hugged the last runner, she came over to me.

"Did you have fun?" Her face was so open, so bright, she seemed illuminated from within, like she'd swallowed a lightbulb. Maybe she just had good skin.

"Yeah," I said. "Quite a fashion show."

"I know, people spend a lot of time looking for the perfect red dress for this run. Did you find any scraps of clothing on the trees in those last two miles of trail? Someone always manages to get a piece of dress ripped off by a branch."

I'd been so busy concentrating on running that if Cinderella's ball gown dyed red had been hanging from a low bough, I probably would have missed it.

"Did you get along with Miles?" When she said this, she cocked her head slightly to the right.

"Um, sure."

"He's a great kid. Oh, shoot," she said. "I have to give him his workout for the week." She pulled a sheet of paper from her jacket. "I can't believe he doesn't have e-mail. Can you give this to him?" She handed me the paper—on which was an incomprehensible script, things like *6 x 800 @ 2:20; 8 tempo; LR (12–13); 3 fartlek*—gave me a hug, and told me to come by the store. Then she flitted off like a tiny running fairy.

People continued to mill around, eating slices of oranges and chunks of bananas and drinking from the same paper cups we'd given out at our—I thought of it as "our"—water station. Everyone still had on their paper numbers and I wondered if any of them would end up on the wall at Joan's store.

It looked like the guys who had mobbed Miles were never going to leave, and I couldn't figure out what to do and felt awkward standing by myself, so I walked over to Miles and shoved the paper at him.

"This is from Joan," I said.

"Hey, thanks." He didn't introduce me to the guys he was talking to and I felt even more awkward.

"She still coaching you?" asked a dude in a shiny strapless prom dress that kept falling down to expose his nipples.

"Wouldn't exactly call it coaching," Miles said. "She writes out a weekly schedule for me. I usually end up doing more than she calls for, but it's good to have a guide."

"Yeah, well, take it with a grain of salt," said the winner.

"Remember the trials—didn't have the guts," chimed in the guy in the wardrobe-malfunctioning prom dress. "But I'm glad she's taken up race directing."

Miles said nothing. He folded and unfolded the sheet of paper I'd given him.

"Gotta go," I said, too loudly and too abruptly.

They all looked at me and I wanted to die.

"Cool hanging with you. See you on the boulevard sometime," Miles said.

5

I could not wait to tell Jenni about my morning activities.

I called her and said, "Come. Over. Now."

"What time is it?" Her voice was soft. I'd probably woken her up.

"Time for you to be up. And for you to get your little self over here."

"Is something wrong? Did you hear from another college?"

Cripes. I'd managed to stop thinking about the whole thing for one morning. Most colleges wouldn't make the decisions until April, or at the very end of March. I still had a lot of waiting to do.

"No, no," I said. "It's all good. Come over. Right. Now." I added, "Please."

"I have to take a shower." She sounded thick and blurry.

"No, no," I said, "you can shower here. You can take a soak if you want." Jenni loved the Jacuzzi tub. "I have something to tell you."

"Okay, okay." She always relented.

I knew Jenni, being Jenni, wouldn't be over for at least forty-five minutes. I was going to burst.

Walter had been awake when I got home. He stood on his back legs and shook the bars of his cage. "You look like a crazed prisoner," I said as I unlatched his door. He climbed out and, as I walked away, ran after me. I waited for him to do what he normally does: make a flying leap and land on my leg like a superhero scaling a tall building. But he didn't.

So I scooped him up and held him to my face.

"Sweetest baby in all the world," I said. "My little honey bunches of oats, my Walter-the-pole-vaulter, my Sir Walter Scott, my poochie snoggins, my Walt-with-no-faults, my bambino lovey-dovey man." He sneezed and his body shook like he was having his own personal earthquake. Then he had to clean his face off so I set him back on the floor.

I was starving, so I went downstairs and, realizing that Jenni probably wouldn't have had breakfast, prepared a plate of her favorite foods: slices of kosher salami, chunks of cheese, a raspberry Pop-Tart (she liked them straight out of the package, unfrosted and not toasted), a handful of potato chips, and a bunch of chocolate-covered Brazil nuts. I made myself some Easy Mac and brought it and Jenni's plate to my room. Walter, who has exquisite taste, also loves Easy Mac. When it had cooled enough, I offered him an elbow.

At first he didn't want it, but eventually he took it.

Before he got down to the business of eating he turned his back on me. He often does this. I give him a piece of food and he pivots to eat it. I'm not sure if it's that he doesn't want to seem rude dining in front of me, or if he thinks I'm going to change my mind and take it away from him.

When he finished, he licked his hands and begged for another piece by standing on his back feet and leaning toward me. He held up one paw and put it on my leg, and I could practically hear him saying, "Please, sir—I want some more" in an Oliver Twist English accent.

"That's enough for now," I said. We both knew that he'd take more elbows but instead of eating them, would stash them somewhere, like inside one of my shoes or in a drawer.

I sat at the computer and searched for Miles. I didn't know his last name. When I Googled "Miles" and "half marathon" about twenty gazillion results came up. I didn't have enough information to be able to stalk—I mean, find out more about—this guy. And I couldn't stop thinking of him.

So instead I did rat Googling.

I found out that rats are both neophobic and neophilic. That means they are afraid of new things (*neophobic*) and also that they love novelty (*neophilia*). Being afraid of new stuff makes sense when people are trying to kill you. Because rats tend to be cautious with any food they haven't had before, they are difficult to poison. I read a bunch about how smart rats are at outfoxing (you might say *out-ratting*) exterminators. If a rat sees one of his friends eat something new and the guy gets sick, he will avoid that food.

Rats are also supposed to be thigmophilic, which means "touch-loving." They don't have the best eyesight, so they rely on touch to navigate, stick near the edges of things, stay on the sides of cages rather than run across the middle. Again, not my experience. If I bring Walt downstairs, or to some unfamiliar place, he might do that initially. Once he realizes he's safe, though, he'll go wherever he wants to, including the middle of the room and onto the lap of whoever's nearby.

He can be a bit of a man-slut, that Walter.

The little dude came over and we had one of our boxing matches where I poke him in the belly with my fingers and he puts up his tiny dukes to fend me off. After a couple of rounds he settled next to me on the bed. I petted his head and he started grinding his teeth—it's called bruxing—and his beautiful black eyes bugged out. He does that when he's relaxed and happy, like a cat purring.

He got so sleepy he ended up on his back with his feet in the air like a baby, but cuter, way cuter, than a human. I moved him over to the pillow and lay down next to him on the bed. I stared at the ceiling and thought about Miles. He was smart and funny and OMG a tasty morsel if I ever saw one. He had been so nice to me.

I thought about the fact that when he realized I didn't have enough breath to run and talk, he did all the talking.

He saved me the embarrassment of having to say any-thing about it—just started yammering away, entertain-ing me, diverting me.

I thought about how, when we were standing next to each other by the table, he had lightly touched me to get my attention when he wanted to point out a particularly funny dress. The place he put his hand—just the top of my shoulder—tingled for the rest of the day. When I thought about it, it tingled again.

Crazy, I know.

I thought about how he had bumped me with his hip at one point, nothing more than a playful tap, but I could feel the warmth of his body, could feel some kind of weird con-nection.

I thought about his hands. His fingers were long, strong. Just like the rest of him. He was narrow, not broad and bulky like that old Kyle, but lean and hard.

And, oh. His legs. His butt.

I thought about how he did this thing with his mouth, kind of like chattering his teeth except it wasn't cold. It was, I realized, a lot like Walter's bruxing. On someone else I might have found it odd, but when Miles did it, he seemed quirky and cute.

I thought about how happy it made me when he smiled. I thought about his mouth.

I surprised myself by thinking about what it would be like to kiss that mouth.

Would I even know how to kiss him, if I ever got the chance?

I thought about that until, an hour and seventeen minutes after I called her, Jenni appeared in my room.

"You call that 'right now'?" I said, and pointed at the clock. "What if I was bleeding to death? Or choking?"

Jenni's eyes, perfectly shadowed and mascaraed, looked a little red.

"Sorry," she said, and dropped her purse on the floor. "Were you?"

"Was I what?"

"Bleeding or choking?"

"No. That's not the point."

"I had to clean up at home. There were beer bottles and cigarette butts and frozen pizza crusts all over the living room."

Her father. Off the wagon.

"And then I had to call Kyle."

I rolled my eyes. She ignored me even though I pointed to myself rolling my eyes, and continued, "Then I had a cup of coffee in the kitchen with your mom."

"Are you kidding me? Not only did I make you breakfast"—I offered her the plate of food—"but I summoned you here because I have something kind of good and a little exciting to tell you—in this time of darkness— and you spend hours talking to her? About what?"

"You know," she said, and shrugged off her sweater, which I recognized as having previously belonged to my mother, "stuff."

"What kind of stuff?"

"Boy stuff," she said. Her left thumbnail was bitten to

the quick. She looked down at it and tucked it into a fist. "Kyle stuff."

I rolled my eyes again, louder.

She looked at me, popped a big hunk of cheese into her mouth, and said, "See. That's why I talk to your mom. Now, let's hear about your 'something kind of good and a little exciting.'"

6

So I told her.

I told her about first seeing Miles on the boulevard with Potato. When I said the dog who looked like Toto was named Potato, Jenni laughed so hard she had a coughing fit and I couldn't be mad at her for being late or for consorting with my mother. I told her how I could hardly talk to Miles at first, but that eventually I got more comfortable.

As I expected, she was all excited about the red dresses and the idea of running skirts and wanted to look online for them; maybe she'd make one for me. It might help me feel better about my thighs.

I said, "Yo, dudette, stop. I didn't get you over here to talk about running skirts."

She looked at the floor and I noticed a smudge of mascara on her cheek.

I said, "I mean, I'll get to that. A running skirt would be great. But first I have to tell you about Miles."

"Miles Harden?" she said.

"*What?* You know him?"

I practically started to shake.

"No," she said, in a calm voice that by contrast made me

sound hysterical. "I wouldn't say I know him, but there's a homeschooled guy named Miles Harden who wins nearly all the local races. Kyle talks about him—says he would be a great running back and could help our guys win the division championship if he enrolled here and was on track and cross-country. But I think a coach went to talk to him two years ago and he said thanks but no thanks."

"That sounds like him," I said.

Then I backpedaled and said, "Well, I don't know him enough to know whether or not that is something he'd say, but it fits with my impression, which is that he's cool and totally mature and polite and humble and smart and funny—"

"Alice!" Jenni said. "You like him!" And for the first time that day, she looked like herself again. She raised her hands and squealed, which scared Walter, who had been crawling around inside her purse. We looked over at the purse and it was like the belly of a pregnant woman when you can see the baby kick. He kept poking his head up and making the purse twitch and bulge.

"Walter," I said, in my serious voice. "Walter!" I clapped my hands, which usually got his attention. But he had some kind of project going on in Jenni's purse and wouldn't come out. When he finally emerged, we saw what he'd been up to. He was carrying a Hershey's with Almonds bar.

"Stop, thief!" I said, as he galloped to the bookcase, one of his favorite places to stash food. The top of my *Collected Works of William Shakespeare* was stained with bits of his collected treats.

"No, little dude," I said, and dashed after him. "Not yours."

The bar was heavy for him to carry in his mouth, and he had it by the middle so it extended far on either side of him. He tried to jump up to the top of the paperback books and kept falling back down. I went over and attempted to grab the candy bar from him, but he held on with his hands and his mouth and squeaked—which he rarely does—in protest. He wanted that chocolate.

"Oh, let him have it," Jenni said. "I keep it for emergencies. Seems like he thinks this is one."

"No, it's too much for him," I said, and tried to yank it loose. He didn't let go and now I held a chocolate bar with a rat dangling from it. I grabbed him, and he used his hands to push me away.

It's hard not to be impressed by so much determination in such a small body.

I opened the wrapper, which had distinctive Walter-holes in it, broke off a small piece, and gave it to him. He charged across the room and into the closet. He went behind the door where I wouldn't be able to see him.

"So," Jenni said. "Miles. You like him!" She smiled and I could see every single one of her small, perfect white teeth. Her tone of voice and that smile made me answer, "No I don't," and revert back to myself at the age when you could call "Not it" by putting your finger on your nose.

Jenni sighed and said, "Okay, you don't like him. How about if I fill up the tub and you can tell me about how much you don't like him while I soak?"

Mom bought all these perfumed, milled, flowered, gold-flecked, herb-infused bath soaps and bath oils and bath gels and bottles of bubbly things and all-natural sponges and weird plastic scrubbing brushes and left them on the tub for me, she said, but they were really for Jenni, who delighted in using them.

Often when Jenni came over she'd take a soak and I'd sit on the toilet or prop myself against the wall, and we'd talk until she started raisining—which is what we call it when your skin turns into a shriveled piece of dried fruit from being in the bath for too long. Walter liked to investigate the bubbles, and once I let him go for a swim. He pooped—just three little ones—and Jenni banned him from the tub forever.

"Tell me," she said, submerged in apricot-scented foam.

I had gotten stuck in my head thinking about Miles, when Jenni splashed me with water.

"So are you going to see him again?"

"I don't know," I said. Because I didn't.

7

The reason Jenni made such a big deal about Miles is that I didn't have much history with boys. Or any history with boys.

This was bothersome, since I'd long ago decided I didn't want to go to Yale with all those sophisticated kids without ever having had any history beyond, of course, watching every episode of *Sex and the City*—which I referred to as "educational programming."

My closest boy encounter happened in eighth grade, with Sam Malouf, now my chief academic rival, when Jenni forced me to go with her to a school dance.

She made me let her put makeup on me. She curled my hair and insisted I wear this flirty dress with boots. When she finished getting me ready, I hardly recognized myself and thought, secretly, I looked good.

Which was nothing compared to what my mom thought. You should have heard her go on and on about how Jenni had brought out my eyes, how she'd really made them pop.

"Oh goody," I said. "My eyes are popping. Just what I always wanted."

Twenty seconds after we arrived in the disco-ball-transformed gym, Jenni got asked to dance, and asked again to dance, and I stood around by myself pretending to read the posters that said *Kissing a Smoker Is like Licking an Ashtray* and *Go Wasps!* and *Wasp Football Schedule* tacked up on the bulletin board. I felt silly in the dress and had to stop myself from rubbing my eyes so I didn't turn into a panda.

And then, Sam Malouf asked me to dance.

I didn't know how to dance and didn't know how to say no, so I mumbled, "I guess," and followed him to the edge of the dance floor. When the song started Sam said, "Oh, man, 'Stairway to Heaven.' This is one of the best songs of all time. I can't believe they're playing it. They never play it."

He put his arms around my waist, and I had mine draped over his shoulders, and it was awkward because I was a lot taller than him, and our whole fronts touched, and I could smell his hair product and body wash, and the song, first just a guitar and it felt like one of those coffee-house soft rock–folk things, then an instrument that sounded like a recorder—the kind of recorder I messed around on when I was little—came in, and Sam pressed close against me and pressed his hands against my back, his breath hot on my neck as he mouthed the words to the song and I tried to figure out what the lyrics were and what they meant and I thought I could feel his heart against my stomach, going like mad, and for a minute I wondered what it would be like if he kissed me because all around us couples were dancing and you could tell some of them were kissing even though they weren't supposed to.

And then, *boing!* He had a woody and it was rubbing against my thigh. Thank god that song only starts out slow. When it got faster and people were rock-and-roll dancing I pulled away from him. Sam was embarrassed and I was embarrassed and we looked off in different directions for the forty-seven minutes it took for that song to be over and when it finally was I said, "Gotta go pee. Thanks." And dashed off into the bathroom and sat and waited for Jenni for another hour or six.

A few weeks later, after I got Walter, I made the mistake of telling Sam Malouf about him. That was also the time it became clear I was better in math. Sam Malouf stopped being nice to me and started calling me Rat Girl.

And that was it. The first and last time I even got close to a boy.

Until I was running in the woods with Miles.

When my heart was beating through my chest and I couldn't catch my breath, and I was listening to him talk about running and about those races that went on for days and I could smell his soap and my sweat and the woods had that musty melty beginning-of-spring dampness, I thought about kissing him.

I could not stop thinking about kissing him.

8

Each day when I went for a run, I looked for Miles and Potato.

I replayed the conversations we'd had and tried to think of witty, sassy things I could have said. Maybe if I'd washed my hair, or at least taken a shower that morning, or put on makeup (or had my mother or Jenni put makeup on me) or worn something other than Dad's stupid sweatshirt and the tights that showed off my thunder thighs, he might have liked me.

As the days after the race passed, the moments of excitement disappeared, and instead I got stuck on my endless loop of rejectedness. I regretted being such a loud-mouth when I applied, telling everyone I would be going to Yale. Even though I knew the odds were against me, I never believed I wouldn't get in.

Walter-the-Man was right. I didn't have a good reason for choosing Yale, but still, being rejected sucked.

I had Googled the Theodore Roosevelt quote about failure that Walter-the-Man threw out at me. I printed it and hung it on my bathroom mirror, after making a minor correction for gender. It read:

It is not the critic who counts; not the person who points out how the strong person stumbles, or where the doer of deeds could have done them better. The credit belongs to the person who is actually in the arena, whose face is marred by dust and sweat and blood; who strives valiantly; who errs, who comes short again and again, because there is no effort without error and shortcoming; but who does actually strive to do the deeds; who knows great enthusiasms, the great devotions; who spends herself in a worthy cause; who at the best knows in the end the triumph of high achievement, and who at the worst, if she fails, at least fails while daring greatly, so that her place shall never be with those cold and timid souls who neither know victory nor defeat.

Each time I went into the bathroom, I reread that quote. My thoughts were kind of random. Like:

1. While blow-drying my hair one morning I realized I didn't know great enthusiasms and great devotions other than wishing that my hair was naturally straight like Jenni's.
2. It occurred to me I might turn out to be one of those timid souls who never know victory. This thought came when I popped a pimple on my nose that hurt like you would not believe. And then it kept bleeding.

3. I wondered if critics were worth anything. I mean, aren't book reviewers and movie columnists useful? Was President Roosevelt even right about that?

4. When I came back from a run covered with sweat, I looked at the quote, and then looked at my face in the mirror and wondered where I could find some dust, and maybe some blood to add to the "marred" effect.

5. As I flossed bits of spinach from my teeth on a night when Dad had made spanakopita for dinner I wondered where you could even find the right arena to enter. Did it require an admission ticket?

6. Mostly I thought about failure. There were so many ways to fail. And old Teddy Roosevelt was saying that the main one came from not trying. It made me think that maybe, like the smart rats who knew to avoid poison, I was neophobic, afraid to try new things. And that maybe, for me, this was not a good thing.

9

Even though it was only the beginning of March, and prom wasn't until May, Jenni had been obsessing about her dress. She came over to show me some sketches.

I said, "You've got two months. The *Project Runway* designers are lucky if they get two days."

"While I appreciate your confidence in me, Al, you may have noticed I haven't been selected to compete on *Project Runway*."

"Yet. Because you haven't applied. You are so much better than so many of them."

"Tell me which of these you like."

She put the black clothbound sketchbook Mom had gotten for her on the bed and flipped through the pages. Walter took that as an invitation: he likes to turn book pages. He put his nose underneath and pushed with his head.

"No!" Jenni said, scaring him so he stood completely still.

"Walter," I said, in the low warning voice Dad sometimes used with me.

"Sorry," she said to him. "I need you not to do that."

He looked apologetic.

Then she said to me, "He's a little skinny?" It was part statement and part question.

"No," I said. "He's perfect, as always."

I scooped him up and put him on my shoulder. He licked his hands and rubbed them over his face. He gave my neck a few licks and settled down to nest under my hair.

The first dress was a gown, close fitted, a jewel-tone blue, strapless, with a high slit up one leg. It was chic and elegant. It looked like a Carolina Herrera, a designer worn by Blake Lively and Amy Adams and Olivia Munn. I only know this because when Jenni is reading my mom's recycled *People* magazines, she points this stuff out to me.

The next few designs were more frilly than what I like—and than what looks good on Jenni, according to her. But she says it's fun to make something with lots of elements.

"Could use some editing," I said. Even though I don't really get what that means, it's something Tim Gunn says a lot.

"You're right. Too much going on in these. Too many ideas."

We came to the last one. It had a deep blue fitted bodice that went straight across, strapless. The bottom part was black, with a bow in the front that didn't look too Glinda-the-Good-Witch, and it had a bit of ruffles, well, not ruffles, more like folds—pleats, they're called pleats—and it flared out at the bottom.

"Jenni Jenni Jenni!" Sometimes, when I get excited, I repeat myself.

She nodded her head. "It's my favorite too. It has a touch of Georgina," she said, referring to "the beautiful Georgina Chapman," designer for Marchesa. It's true Georgina Chapman, one of the judges on *Project Runway All Stars*, is gorgeous, but it bugs me that Heidi Klum always uses that adjective to refer to this woman who is smart, and creative, and a shrewd businessperson.

Jenni scrutinized the sketch as if it had been done by someone else. She is able to separate herself from her work in a way that allows her to be self-critical. It's something that we notice many of the *Project Runway* designers can't do. They fall in love with their own ideas, get too attached, and don't see how much trouble they're getting into. It's worst when Tim Gunn points out something. When he says, "This worries me," and furrows his brow and cocks his left arm, they should know they're headed for a crash. If he then says, "Carry on," and walks away, and they keep doing what they were doing, we cringe.

I feel like I've learned a lot from *Project Runway* about the importance of being able to take criticism.

I also know I'm not so good at it.

The only person I showed my college-application essay to was Walter-the-Man. After I finished, I was proud of it. Of course, I'm usually proud of whatever I do right after I do it. I've learned I generally need to let something sit for a while to be able to see its flaws and weaknesses, but I was confident I was going to get into Yale. I dashed off the essay, thought it was great, and then, because I wanted praise and not feedback, I brought it down to Walter-the-Man one day when he was watching a football game and said, "Read this."

He didn't look up from the TV screen.

"Halftime."

So I sat and flipped through *The New Yorker*, noticing for the zillionth time that I never think the cartoons are funny, and listened to him scream—at the referees and at the players on his team and at the players on the other team and at the TV cameraman and at the ad people who made the commercials—for about seven hours.

After I had to listen to him recap the whole first half for me, I said, "Do I look like I care?"

He said, "No, but you do look like someone who wants a favor and, if that's the case, you might want to indulge the person from whom you want something."

Then he read the essay.

When he finished, Walter-the-Man was quiet for a long time. He was almost never quiet. He put down the pages and looked at me.

"What I understand from Deborah is that the essay isn't an essential part of the application process. A bad essay won't keep you out if you've got a lot of other things going for you. But a good essay can help illuminate aspects that don't show up anywhere else. Deborah says most essays are bland and typical."

I waited for him to tell me how good it was and maybe to point out a typo or a missing word.

He seemed uncomfortable. He said, "This essay is bland and typical. I don't see enough of the Alice I know—and sometimes like—in it. It's called a personal statement, but there's nothing really and truly personal in it."

I sat for another minute, said, "Thank you for your opinion," grabbed the paper back, and went up to my room.

10

Walter-the-Man acted like he had the inside scoop and was an expert on admissions. He tended to *mansplain*. That should be an SAT word. It means "to explain something with complete and utter confidence even if you don't know what you're talking about." In fairness, it's not only men who do this. I think sometimes I may be guilty of mansplaining.

I don't know why Walter-the-Man was so interested in the whole admissions thing—he didn't have any kids and the only non-middle-aged person he knew was me. When I was younger, Mom kept saying we were going to need him "in a couple of years" and she'd tilt her head in my direction. I only half listened to the stories because they seemed so crazy.

According to Deborah as channeled by Walter-the-Man, the numbers were stacked against the applicants and no one could count on getting in. She said although 80 percent of the kids could do the work if they were admitted, they accepted more like 20 percent. She said you could take the entire first-year class, wipe it out, and se-

lect one just as good from the pool of those who'd been rejected for the same class.

She said all the kids looked alike. They all took the
same courses, got the same grades and test scores. They
were all at the top of their class, all National Merit Schol-
ars; they all excelled and exhibited leadership in the same
extracurricular activities, and they even wrote their essays on similar topics. The dead-grandma essay. The
baseball = life riff.

One of the things Deborah said, according to Walter-
the-Man, was that top schools weren't looking for well-
rounded kids; they wanted a well-rounded class. This
meant they were more inclined to take applicants who
were "angular" or "well lopsided," people who had gotten
interested in something and pursued it to the nth degree.

My application to Yale—and the applications I had sub-
mitted at the last minute to the other colleges that would
no doubt REJECT me in April—probably made me look as
typical as you could get. Except I was worse than typical.
I lacked the expected laundry list of extracurricular activities. I had shown no leadership. I had founded no organizations. I had not written a novel or discovered a protein.
I had not tried to broker a peace treaty between Israel and
Palestine.

And I wrote my essay about how much I hated *The
Catcher in the Rye*. I thought it was ironic that Holden
goes around calling everyone a phony when he's the biggest

phony of them all. He's nice and polite to people but all he does is pass judgment on them. He's a pissed-off little asshole. No one wants to hang out with someone who's crabby all the time.

I should know. These days I can't even stand to be with myself.

It had been three weeks since the Red Dress Run, with no Miles/Potato sightings. So I decided to run along Quarrier toward downtown.

Maybe it was the change in route, or maybe the wind was at my back, or maybe—could it be?—I was getting better, but OMG it felt effortless. My legs didn't hurt and my breathing was normal and I was covering ground like I never had before. I was able to keep it up for a long time without slowing down, not like my short sprints where I'd run fast for a block and then have to pant bent over with my hands on my knees. I could keep up this pace for a while. It was amazing.

After getting chased by a golden retriever for about two blocks—I didn't feel threatened, since he was wagging his tail and carrying a rawhide bone—and having an old couple out walking tell me that I was a good girl for getting exercise, I ended up at Joan's store. I figured I might take a look to see what kind of running equipment was available. It was after school, around 4:30 on Wednesday, and there weren't many people around. When I walked in, the store was completely empty. The bell on the door jingled, but still, nothing.

I waited for a few minutes and thought I'd open the door again, but then Joan popped out from behind a curtain carrying four boxes of shoes that rose above her head.

I coughed, not wanting to scare her, and she dropped the boxes.

"Sorry," I said, and went to help her restack.

"Alice! Great to see you! I didn't hear you come in. I've been dealing with inventory that's backing up because I lost—" And she stopped and looked at me.

"You lost?" I let my question trail off, thinking about the conversation I'd overheard at the race and wondering what she was going to say next.

"Hey," she said, standing up straight and putting her hands on her tiny waist. I could see her thinking. "You got any spare time?"

I lowered my head in a slow nod.

"I lost one of my part-time employees—he decided to go live at altitude and train in Flagstaff, Arizona. He was only working a few hours a few days a week and I thought I'd be fine without him, but"—she swept an arm toward the boxes on the floor—"it turns out I was wrong. Interested in coming in Wednesday afternoons and Saturday mornings for a couple hours?"

A job? In the summer I sometimes stopped in at my dad's law office and helped out by filing papers and making copies and scanning materials. I hadn't ever had a real job.

"It's not glamorous. Mostly unpacking merchandise, logging inventory, pricing things, restocking, and tidying up the store." She looked at me apologetically and said, "Plus some vacuuming and taking out the trash."

I said, "Trash is something I can do."

"You'll be able to pick up a lot of useful information. And you'll get to know the local running community because, sooner or later, everyone comes into the store."

She stepped around the boxes, shoved the curtain aside, and showed me into the stockroom, which was stuffed with more boxes and clothes in plastic wrappers. "It's a bit of a mess right now," she said.

"Yes," I said, and then I caught myself. "I mean, not yes it's a mess," though of course, it was. "Yes, I'd love to work here. I mean, I'll have to ask my parents, but I'm sure it will be fine."

"Fabulous!" Joan said in her exclamation-pointed voice. "It will only be until June when my regulars come back from college. I promised the kids who've worked for me during high school they'll always have a summer job here if they want it. But still, nothing will make you feel more like a runner than hanging around with other runners. That's one of the things that separates us from the joggers. It's not speed. It's that—" and she pointed to the back wall of the store, which had all the pieces of paper with big block numbers on them.

Then she looked at me with an impish smile and said, "Did you have fun with Miles at the Red Dress Run?"

"Sure," I said, and quickly pointed to the back wall to distract her from this sensitive territory. "So what's up with that?"

It worked. She turned and left the subject of Miles.

"That's my favorite part of the store. After we'd been open for a while, and people would come in and tell us about their races, I decided to create a place for them to share their achievements. I ask folks to bring in the bibs from their first race—or the race that made them start to think of themselves as runners, or the race where they ran their PR."

She must have seen my confusion because she said, "A PR is a personal record—the fastest time you've run in a given event. These are all from races customers have run. I encourage them to write their name on the number, to show everyone they've done it, they made it to the starting line. That's what it's all about as far as I'm concerned. Getting to the start. Once the gun goes off, experienced racers know anything can happen. You could have stomach problems. It can be crazy hot. Or start pouring rain. You might be getting a cold. Or getting over one. You could just have a bad day. Someone else could be having a great one. But if you can get yourself to the start line, you've made it. After that, there is no failure."

We had moved over to the wall, blanketed thick with these numbers. She said, "Some folks write down the words or phrases that helped get them through the race."

I saw lots of them:

My sport is what yours does for punishment
I did it!
Do or Do Not. There is No Try
Failure is not an option
Tall and strong
What doesn't kill me makes me stronger
Stay focused
Kick butt
Running is my happy hour
Pain is temporary but pride is forever
Never give up
Hills are my friend
Pain is what I have for breakfast
Pain is weakness leaving the body
Pain feels so much better than regret
Pain now beer later
Unbreakable
This is exactly where I want to be
Mitochondria, not hypochondria
I'll rest when I'm dead
If it was easy everyone would do it
A hero holds on one minute longer
The body achieves what the mind believes
When your legs give out, run with your heart
Today is my day
I think I can I think I can I think I can
I will survive

Dig deeper
One mile at a time
Fast feet
Run like a girl
Never back down
I could do this all day long
I run for chocolate
I am a runner
Believe
Endure
Flow
Breathe
Run

Some of the numbers said, *In memory of* or *In honor of* and there were names. *Mom. Dad. My uncle Tim. Aunt Mary. Grandma. Grandpa. Rusty. Jean. David. William. Michelle. Ricardo.* There were lots and lots of numbers that said *Ricardo.*

Joan saw me looking at them.

"Ricardo, my late husband," she said. "I'll tell you about him sometime."

12

Because I had run to the store, I had to run back home, and even though I was excited about my new job—we decided my first day would be Saturday morning—it was hard to start running again after standing around inside for so long. After my *exultant* ("triumphantly happy") dash through downtown on the way there, I ended up having to switch off walking and running to get back and it took a long time.

When I got home my father and Jenni were skittering around the kitchen. They had a zillion pots on the stove and Jenni wore cake batter on her cheek.

Dad said, "Finally."

Jenni said, "Did you forget?"

"Forget what?"

"She forgot," Jenni said to Dad, and he gave me a look that made me feel small. Dad doesn't have to say much for me to know when I've disappointed him.

"Your mom's birthday? We're making her favorite foods? You were supposed to pick up some bacon chocolate bars. That was your idea—what you thought you could contribute."

Crap. Double-triple-cherry-on-top crap. There had been a lot of discussion about what to do for my mother's birthday. Jenni had a ton of ideas and she and Dad had been planning it for weeks. While they were having these conversations I wouldn't really listen but would frequently point out that I had nothing to contribute.

Jenni finally said I was being a pill and could I please at least pretend to be interested. Eventually I said since Mom liked bacon and chocolate, I would get her some of these fancy candy bars that combined them. And now I'd totally forgotten.

I'd also forgotten to get her a gift.

"Oops," I said.

Dad looked at me again for a minute, shook his head, and went back to his root vegetables. My mom loves this thing he makes that's potatoes with parsnips and rutabagas mixed in. He bakes it with a crust of Parmesan cheese and bread crumbs on top. A mush of white vegetables with white cheese.

Yummy.

Not.

"It's okay," said Jenni. "You can help me with the cake."

When Jenni and I first started watching the TV show *Cake Boss*, she was all about learning how to make fondant, the moldable icing the cake boss used like clay. We got the ingredients and she spent a lot of time messing around with them. You make it into a big sheet, and you can cut, roll, or shape it into whatever you want.

For my birthday last year, she made a cake that looked like the bottom of Walter's cage. It had a fondant replica of his sleeping hut, his food bowl, chunks of his pellets (made from ground nuts and honey, which he preferred to his real food), and a perfect likeness of the little dude himself. I brought him downstairs and allowed him to eat part of his fondant tail, which was:

1. Cleaner than the real thing.
2. Kind of gross to watch him eating something that looked so real.
3. Delicious.

"Gotta get Walter," I said, and before Dad could turn around to look at me again, I ran upstairs. I heard Jenni calling after me but I pretended I didn't.

When I got to my room, I stripped off my running clothes, opened Walter's cage, and hopped into the shower. I couldn't believe I had forgotten about my mother's birthday because it was a big deal for her.

She didn't like getting older, but she did like a celebration and she loved it when my dad cooked.

When I was a kid, I refused to eat my dad's food. There's usually too much going on. The potatoes are a perfect example. Why couldn't he make plain old smashed potatoes like the ones they served in the school cafeteria? Why did he have to go and put in those other weird vegetables? I mean, have you seen a parsnip? It looks like a deformed albino carrot, pale and sickly.

When I had a box of Kraft macaroni and cheese at Jenni's house for the first time, I knew I'd found the foundation of my food pyramid. That's what her father cooked for dinner nearly every night after her mom died, until Jenni learned to cook on her own. I envied her. Then I discovered Easy Mac—which Jenni says her dad says is too expensive—and that's my go-to meal and snack. It drives Dad nuts. He offers to make me real mac and cheese, the kind with creamy béchamel goo and funky stinky Gruyère, and I respond by sticking a finger in my throat and making gagging noises. Dad doesn't get too upset, but it bothers Mom. So she compensates by making a big deal of what a great cook he is and eating more than I know she wants. My dad measures how much you like his food by the quantity you eat.

When I got out of the shower, Walter was waiting for me in the bathroom, doing laps around the toilet. He likes to lick my legs dry. He starts with the tops of my feet and works his way up my ankles. He has plenty of water in his cage, so it's not like he's thirsty.

"Okay, that's enough." I dragged the towel in front of him and he chased it, and I slowed it down and he pounced and landed on it and I zoomed him around on the towel and said, "Sleigh ride!" He got bored with the game before I did and jumped off. Then he had a sneezing fit.

I went into my closet—he followed right behind me— and put on my holey jeans and a sweatshirt that had a psycho bunny on it. I perched Walter on my shoulder and went back downstairs.

When I came into the kitchen Jenni looked at me and said, "You're going to change before dinner, right?" She knew how much Mom hated those Walter-enhanced jeans.

"Maybe. Hey, pied beauty, you want a piece of parsnip?" I headed over to Dad's side of the kitchen. He and Jenni had separate work spaces—his was by the stove and she had used the counter to lay out all her materials.

Jenni grabbed me by the arm and said, "You stay over here. If you're not going to help, don't get in the way. Be a fountain not a drain, Alice."

Dad, who was chopping something, rocked out to Bruce Springsteen.

"Geez, who's in charge around here?" I said, gathering up a bunch of cake crumbs, rolling them into a ball, and popping the whole thing into my mouth. I made a smaller ball and gave it to Walter.

13

As it turned out, I continued to be more of a drain than a fountain.

Walter jumped off my shoulder, onto the counter, and ran across the top of the cake.

Dad shouted, "Alice!"

Jenni tried not to be mad, but he had left some footprints. ("Leave only footprints" may be a good motto when you're hiking in the woods, but not so much when you're running across a birthday cake.) I said, "You're going to put icing on it, right?"

When I wasn't looking, Walt nibbled on a leather case Mom used for spare keys. By the time I caught him, he'd already made substantial progress. He jumped to the floor, ran to the refrigerator, and I had to scream at Dad not to step on him.

Dad got mad and said, "Take that rat upstairs. Now."

No one is ever supposed to refer to Walter as "that rat"—it's dehumanizing. Almost as bad as calling him "it." If someone responds to his own name, it shows a sense of self, and he deserves to be treated as someone with a self. But I knew it probably wasn't a good time to have this discussion with my father so I grabbed Walt and brought him back to his cage.

I stayed upstairs for a while trying to figure out a gift for my mother. I decided to give her a novel, since she mostly reads serious books—biographies and bestsellers that explain big ideas in economics or science. I thought it would be good for her to read some fiction.

When I was little, to encourage me to read, my parents made me a promise: they would buy me any book I wanted. I'm not sure they realized I was going to want books more than clothes, or shoes, or even a pony, though I did want a pony for a long time and finally had to settle for weekly riding lessons. A couple of years ago they bought me an e-reader and said I could use their credit card to download any book. But I hardly used it.

While I appreciate the convenience of electronic versions, I love real books, the smell of them, the way they feel in my hands.

About once a month Dad and I go to a local bookstore. Dad says bookstores are staffed with supersmart people who believe that literature matters and that if you can find someone who either knows or shares your taste, they can be a great resource. So I look for books recommended by the staff, especially Barbara and Garth, read the descriptions on the back covers, and get anything that looks good. I leave the store with big bags and I stack the books up on the floor next to my bed. Whenever the stack starts getting too small, I freak out, and we have to go get more. I always need to have a big TBR (to be read) pile. When I finish books, I move them to the bookcase, where Walter sometimes nibbles the edges or stores food along the tops.

I scanned my shelves to figure out which one I could give to Mom. Maybe it's a little tacky to give someone a previously owned book, but it's not like they get used up in the reading. So I considered my options:

Pride and Prejudice. No. She must have read it at some point. Who hasn't?

The Things They Carried. No. A book about war could send the wrong message, though it's really about love and friendship and is totally awesome. I'm not sure if it's fiction or nonfiction.

The Curious Incident of the Dog in the Night-Time. Maybe. Mom always says she doesn't like murder mysteries, but in this one the person who gets murdered is a poodle, and the detective is a fifteen-year-old boy who's maybe got Asperger's. Plus, he has a pet rat named Toby. Not many novels with sympathetic rat characters.

Stargirl. No. We read this together when I was a kid. But I love it so much.

Where the Wild Things Are. Ditto.

The Hunger Games. No. Even though the book is a zillion times better than the movie, I'm pretty sure that, based on her reaction to the movie, Mom wouldn't want to read it. She didn't like the idea of kids killing kids. I said it wasn't at all surprising: kids are vicious, if she hadn't noticed.

The Collected Poems of Emily Dickinson. No. I didn't want to give up my copy, especially since Walter-the-Man told me that you could sing all of her poems to the tune of "The Yellow Rose of Texas." I often sang "Because I could not stop for Death" to Walter.

Then I saw the perfect gift book.

Of course, I didn't have any wrapping paper in my room, so I cut out pages from one of Mom's *People* magazines and made a collage of photos of the lips of different movie stars—which even I could tell had been pumped up with collagen—and taped it together with Band-Aids. I thought this was a clever commentary on my mother's chosen profession.

Then, since I didn't have a card, I folded a piece of paper in half, wrote on the front, *This is a card*, and scrawled *Happy Birthday, old girl. XO, A* inside. I was quite pleased with myself when I went back downstairs to the kitchen, where Jenni and Dad scurried around like busy mice.

The main dish was Cornish game hens, because Mom loved them. She said her mother always used to make them on special occasions. I like them because they're like mini-chickens, and as everyone knows, I love all things mini.

Dad had finished putting stuffing in their body cavities and was slopping some kind of orangey sauce on their skin.

"What is a Cornish game hen, anyway?" I asked, as I stuck my finger into the batter Jenni was mixing. After all these years of eating them, I'd never really thought about what they were other than Cornishgamehens. Like the way you don't think about the lyrics of songs like "America the Beautiful" as meaningful words. They're just

Obeautifulforspaciousskies and *Forpurplemountainmajes-ties*. Purple mountain majesties?

"It's a bird."

"I know that. Is it just a mini-chicken?"

"No," he said. "It's a different species. You know—there are turkeys and ducks and chickens and Cornish game hens."

He said it with such certainty I felt compelled to check. I whipped out my iPhone and Googled.

"Ahem," I said. "From *Wikipedia*: 'A Cornish game hen . . . is a hybrid chicken sold whole. Despite the name, it is not a game bird, but actually a type of domestic chicken. Though the bird is called a "hen," it can be either male or female.'"

Dad said nothing. Jenni didn't look up from the cake.

"So," I said, "a Cornish game hen is not Cornish, not game, and not even a hen. It is, in fact, a mini-chicken."

"Nice, Alice," Jenni said, still not looking up, as she greased the pan.

14

In addition to the regulars—Jenni and Walter-the-Man—Sylvia and Gary came over for dinner. They had both gone to medical school with Mom. Sylvia was my mom's best friend, an oncologist, and Gary was a radiologist.

Jenni had set the table. She folded the napkins into swans. She filled vases with marbles and made a "flower" arrangement using vegetables: radishes morphed into roses under her knife, carrots turned into happy daisies, and green onions served as leafery. She had found this cool centerpiece—Dad said it had been a wedding present—and filled it up with tall skinny white candles. She had also printed menu cards and placed them in front of each person's plate:

Wild mushroom toast points
Shaved fennel salad
Cornish game hens
Roasted asparagus with lemon-and-thyme butter
Smashed root vegetables
Meyer lemon sorbet
BlackBerry cake

I thought the last item might have been a mistake so I asked her about it. I had, after all, been eating balls of smushed-up chocolate-cake crumbs.

"Nope," she said. "Blackberry cake."

Jenni asked me to set out wineglasses for red and white wines, plus the champagne flutes. Seriously, our dining room had never looked this fancy. I decided to change my clothes when I saw that Jenni had put on a black cashmere sweaterdress that came from the Jenni Sack—Mom had bought it "by mistake" and had "gotten the wrong size" and "couldn't be bothered to return it." It was Jenni's favorite item of clothing ever.

Mom knew we were making dinner for her. She hated surprises. We'd learned that the hard way a few years ago. But when she got home from work and saw the dining room, she went straight to Jenni and put her arm around her. "My girl," she said.

After everyone was seated, after lots of oohing and aahing about how beautiful the table looked, Dad lifted his champagne glass and said, "To Sarah."

Mom had declared no birthday candles and said we weren't allowed to sing "that song." She always said, "I can't stand that song."

But I started to sing it anyway.

Jenni kicked me under the table.

"What?" I said.

Dad interrupted and said, again, "To Sarah."

Gary said, "Yes, to Sarah." And raised his glass. "The smartest woman I knew at Duke."

Mom put down her glass, leaned across the table, and said, "What do you mean?"

Gary said, "What do you mean what do I mean? What I said. You were the smartest woman I knew at Duke."

Mom tried to raise her eyebrow. She couldn't and instead widened her eyes and said, "Tell me, Gary, what man at Duke was smarter than me?"

Everyone laughed and Mom looked really happy.

Sylvia raised her glass and said, "To the smartest person we knew at Duke," and everyone drank. I took a few gulps, but it's not that much fun to drink with your parents, especially if they give you permission. Jenni doesn't like alcohol, what with her dad and all, but she had one sip after the toast.

Jenni was up and down all night, filling people's glasses, bringing in food from the kitchen. At one point, I saw my mother take hold of her arm and squeeze it. The look that passed between them made me feel invisible.

Sylvia started to ask me a question but I was afraid it was going to be about college so I cut her off, saying, "Isn't it time for cake?"

It wasn't.

So we sat there for a while longer and finally Jenni went into the kitchen to get dessert and I trailed behind her saying that I would help. We both knew I wasn't going to help.

Jenni had covered the cake with a dish towel. When she pulled it off, I gasped. I actually gasped.

Jenni has made some great cakes, but this one was *Cake Boss*–worthy.

It was, in fact, a BlackBerry cake. That is, it was a cake that looked exactly like Mom's BlackBerry. We had tried to get her to switch to an iPhone, like a normal person. She resisted, saying she loved her BlackBerry, loved the keyboard, loved the way it felt in her hand. Jenni had created a cake shaped like something my mother loved.

She'd used edible paper to put the letters on each key and to write the "e-mail" message on the screen: *Happy Birthday Sarah. We love you.* She'd done all of this since Walter had run across the top. I thought it was just going to be a plain chocolate cake.

Jenni carried the cake to the dining room and placed it in front of my mother, who threw her head back and laughed and laughed. She stood up—nearly pushing her chair over—and hugged Jenni so hard I could practically hear the whoosh of breath leaving Jenni's lungs.

We all applauded.

"Now, presents," Jenni said, clapping her hands so that only the palms touched, like a seal catching a ball.

Dad slipped a box from Mom's favorite jewelry store in front of her. For years they'd had a joke, "Where's the box?" On her birthday, or during Hanukah, Dad would give Mom these nice, practical gifts—like a GPS for her car, or an iPod preloaded with her favorite tunes, or once, and this was a low point, an automatic hot-water dispenser for the kitchen. Mom, who always complains about being cold when the temperature dips below eighty-four degrees, drinks gallons of hot water with lemon at practically every meal, and she hates waiting for the teakettle to boil. Even the microwave is too slow for her. So Dad had installed the InSinkErator.

But when he brought my mom into the kitchen and showed it to her, she said, "That's great, Matt. Love it. But you don't get someone hot water for her birthday. Now. Where's the box?"

This time, though, there was a box. A tiny, exquisite suede box. Mom opened it, snapped it closed, and threw her arms around Dad. "Oh, Matt," she said.

Sylvia said, "Pass it over," and my mom handed her the box. Sylvia took out a small gold ring with a stone the color of royalty.

"Tanzanite," Mom said.

"And this," Dad said, handing her a shoe box wrapped in shiny silver paper with a big blue bow. "Sorry—I can't stop being me."

She opened it to find a dozen pairs of reading glasses. Mom was always losing her reading glasses. "Now you can leave them all over the house and office," Dad said.

Sylvia grabbed one of the pairs of glasses, put them on, and inspected the ring. "This is gorgeous, Matt. Nice job."

"I had some help," he said, and looked over at Jenni.

Christ on a bike! How much planning and shopping and colluding had these people done?

Sylvia gave Mom a gift certificate to a spa and said they were going to have a pampering day together.

Walter-the-Man handed over a card, and when my mom opened it, three tickets to a Gillian Welch show fluttered out. Mom, Jenni, and I all love Gillian Welch.

"Girls' night," Walter-the-Man said. "I'll babysit Matt." And he mouthed to my dad, *NC State game.*

Jenni's present was something she must have spent the past few weeks in shop class working on: a makeup mirror. It was carved out of some dark hardwood, and she had done the electrical work so it had a light built in. Part of it was regular mirror, and part was magnifying. The detail was intricate, delicate, and elegant.

Then it was my turn. I handed over a paperback book published in 2000, the cover of which had been nibbled by a rat, wrapped in pages torn from a magazine and held together with Band-Aids, along with a card that could have been made by an eight-year-old. Jenni looked horrified.

My mother read the title out loud: *A Heartbreaking Work of Staggering Genius.*

I said, "It's a true story. Both of his parents died of cancer when he was a senior in college and he had to take care of his little brother. It's really funny."

Sylvia put a hand on my mother's back.

"That's very nice, Alice. Thank you," Mom said, and the room got quiet.

Jenni's face was white.

Dad was staring into his cake plate and shaking his head. He looked up at me and said, "What is wrong with you?"

"It's really funny," I said in a weak voice.

15

The grownups escaped into the living room to talk and drink more wine, leaving me and Jenni to clean up. Jenni stacked the plates aggressively and practically threw the silverware into the dishwasher.

I said, "I think I'll get Walter to help us with this."

She stopped, bent over the sink, and said without turning around, "Can you think about somebody other than yourself for one minute?"

"What do you mean? I was thinking about Walter."

"You know, Alice, I've listened to you whine about Yale. Everyone has listened to you whine about Yale. You work so hard on your vocabulary. Do you know the meaning of the word *self-absorbed*? How about *self-centered*? How about just plain *inconsiderate*?"

I looked at her. Jenni was never mean and rarely angry, but now she hissed at me.

"Your dad worked really hard on this dinner and you couldn't even remember it was your mom's birthday. All you think about is yourself. And then you give her that crummy old book. Did you also manage to forget that your mother's mom died of cancer when she was in college?"

I hadn't even thought of that. It was just a really good book. I said, "But it's funny."

Jenni was trembling and her lower lip started to quiver. Her voice got soft and she said, "And another thing."

It's never a good thing in an argument when someone says, "and another thing." I braced myself.

"Do you realize that in all our conversations about college, you haven't once asked me what I'm planning to do next year."

Crap.

She was right.

I hadn't brought it up because school never seemed important to her. Jenni cared about cheerleading and dances and the right color of lip gloss.

"I—I didn't think—"

"Right. You didn't think. So you know what? In July I'm moving to New York City."

"What?"

"Your mom got me an internship with a designer she knows from college."

How could this be? I hadn't heard anything about it.

Jenni continued. "I'm going to work for a year, live in Brooklyn as a nanny with another friend of your mom's from medical school, and then apply to FIT or maybe Parsons the following year. Your mom has made all of this possible for me."

Jenni was going to apply to Parsons?

"We all tiptoe around you because we love you. And we forgive you for being so self-involved because we know that's how you are. But it would be nice if you could at least sometimes, for a few minutes, notice that there are other people in the world."

She dried her hands on a towel and walked out, leaving me to finish the dishes.

16

Jenni avoided me at school the rest of the week. Mom and Dad were annoyed with me, so when I got home I just went up to my room and stayed there. I read e. e. cummings's poems out loud to Walter and I repeated the line, "nobody, not even the rain, has such small hands" five times. I played a lot of Freerice.

It wasn't that different from what I usually did, but I felt awful. I didn't mean to be self-involved and inconsiderate. I didn't mean to forget Mom's birthday or keep putting off asking Jenni about her plans for next year. It wasn't like I didn't care. I just got stuck in my own head, mired in my own muck.

On Saturday, I started working at Joan's store, Runner's Edge, which Mom referred to as "Joan's store" and I guess I picked that up from her.

The stockroom, littered with piles of boxes and plastic bags containing shirts and shorts, needed help. I sat on the floor and put everything into neat stacks so I could use the fun machine that made price tags. After a couple of hours, the piles were a lot smaller. Occasionally I'd bring merchandise to Joan and she'd put it on hangers on the round racks.

A compact woman with thick red corkscrew hair burst through the door and shouted, "Hi honey, I'm home!"

"Nikki!" Joan said.

"Yo." These two tiny chicks gave each other a chest bump—as if they were basketball players.

The woman told Joan she needed a new pair of shoes and wanted to try something with a lower profile. "I'm not ready to join the barefoot craze," she said, "but, well, I don't know, I wondered if there was maybe some middle ground."

"I have something I think you'll like, Nik," Joan said, and went into the stockroom.

"Great," said the woman. She had been wearing hiking boots and now she peeled off thick wool socks.

Her feet were even uglier than mine, if you can believe that. A couple of her toes curled down and her two big toenails were purple. Not painted purple, like with nail polish, but the nails themselves.

"What?" she said, when she saw me looking at them. "Never seen a runner's feet before?"

I said, "First day on the job." Then I felt really awkward so I said, "Um, can I offer you a Tootsie Roll?" Joan kept a big jar of candy on the front counter. She said runners really liked candy. From what I'd seen that morning, it was Joan who really liked candy.

Joan came out with two boxes of shoes and said, "They

run small, so I brought you a 9 as well as an 8½. And here's a pair of socks." She tossed them at Nikki.

Joan lifted her chin in my direction and said, "Alice just started running. She's learning."

Then she turned to me and explained, "Many runners end up with black toenails from blood blisters that form under the nail bed. Sometimes they're the result of wearing shoes that are too small, but usually, especially for experienced runners like Nikki, they're the price of doing business. Nikki is a fast downhill runner, and the foot naturally slides forward in the shoe. There's nothing dangerous about them—"

"They hurt like mofos," Nikki said.

"—but they don't make for pretty feet. Eventually, they fall off."

"The toenail falls off?" I blurted out. "That's disgusting."

I realized too late that may not have been the most polite thing to say. But both Joan and Nikki were laughing.

"Yep," said Nikki. "Usually by that time, a new one has begun to grow underneath. I have a collection of them at home in a bowl in the guest bathroom."

Nikki put on the new shoes, got up, and walked around. She jumped up and down a few times. She said, "I rarely have ten toenails at one time. Wow. This feels strange. Kind of like wearing Earth Shoes. Remember Earth Shoes, Joan, where the heel was lower than the front? I'm tipping backward." And she rocked back as if she was going to fall.

"They're cushioned, superlight, and I think for the kind of running you do, both roads and trails, they might work well. Take them out for a spin."

Nikki ran out the door. Joan said to me, "Wait until you see the hammer toes. And the bunions. And the blisters—you've never seen blisters until you see someone who's had a rough race. The whole bottom of the foot can be one giant blister."

I must have made a face because she said, "We think of them as badges of honor, along with our cuts and bruises and scrapes. It's because we're out mixing it up. If you run hard, you might fall. If you fall, you might get dirty, a little bloody. Nothing too bad. Most serious injuries come from overuse."

Nikki burst back into the store. "Yes!" she said. "Love them."

"Thought you might," said Joan, and she moved to the register. I followed and watched her ring up the sale. She said, "Charleston Running Club members get a 10 percent discount." I knew about the club from the Red Dress Run.

"Also need something for chub rub," Nikki said.

Joan said to me, "Body Glide," and motioned to an item on the wall rack that looked like a stick of deodorant. "Chafing," she explained, and pointed in the direction of her inner thighs. Then she yelped, "Nikki! I forgot! How was your marathon?"

Nikki put her hands into her head of curls and groaned. "You don't want to know."

"What happened? You were shooting for sub–2:50, right?"

"That was the plan. You know what happens when people plan. God laughs. At my race, she laughed so hard she probably peed her pants."

"Your training went so well."

"Yeah, but my racing didn't go well that day. I got behind on calories. I was feeling good, running fast, but I didn't take in enough fuel. I bonked. Hit the wall at 25."

Bonked? I thought. Hit the wall? There's a wall? Near the end of a marathon?

Joan looked at me and said, "That's a saying. Not a literal wall."

"Sure feels like it. I was on pace through 24 and a half. Then the wheels came off. I could not get my legs to move. There was nothing I could do to change my fate."

"Glycogen debt," Joan said. "Been there."

"I never had been before. It sucked. There were so many spectators, and I was the first woman, and they were all cheering me on but when I got to the mile marker at 25, I had nothing left. And after that, you're beyond all help. Gatorade or gel or salt tabs—nothing does any good. It's all muscling and mentalling it out and I couldn't do it. I finished in 2:57. Humiliated."

I had some thoughts:

1. Seven minutes were that big a deal?
2. It seemed silly to be able to run at mile 24 but not at mile 25. I mean, you've already run that many miles. What's one more?

3. I felt like I'd been stuck in my own version of
mile 25 since I'd been rejected from Yale.

"So sorry, Nik," Joan said. "We've all been there. Sometimes you're the windshield, sometimes you're the bug."

"I was beyond insectitude at that point. I was slime. I
was primordial ooze. But I'm back at it."

"Box?" Joan called. Nikki had picked out packets of gel
in different flavors and flipped them onto the counter.

"No thanks," she said, "but I need to stock up on por-
table calories."

Joan handed me the empty shoe box and I brought it
back into the stockroom. Then the front door jingled and I
heard Joan say, "Miles!"

Without moving a muscle, without breathing, I listened.

"Hey, kid," I heard Nikki say. "You here to pick up your
weekly recipe for speed?"

"Know it," Miles said in the easiest, most comfortable
voice. "You chicked me once. Not going to happen again."

"We'll see about that," Nikki said.

"I hate that word," Joan said. "The idea of getting
'chicked' is ridiculous. We are competing in different races.
If a woman beats a man and wins overall, she still gets the
trophy with the boobs. She's still only First Woman, not
Overall Winner. So why is getting beaten by a woman any
big thing? Why do so many men care about beating the first
woman? You're competing against other men, Miles; Nikki
is competing against other women. When she beats you—"

"You've been chicked," Nikki said with a laugh, "and you will be again."

"Argh," said Joan.

I heard Nikki thank Joan, tell Miles she'd see him around, and leave the store. I didn't want to come out of the stockroom. Then Joan called my name.

17

When I finally emerged, Miles was standing there, in short shorts and a long-sleeved T-shirt that said *Jingle Bell 10K*. He'd obviously been running.

Joan said, "You remember Miles."

"Um, sure."

"Alice. Hey."

Awkward, I thought.

Joan said, "I need to dash over to the bank for a minute. Will you take the helm?" She grabbed a cloth envelope from the safe, stuffed most of the bills from the register into it, and pranced out the door.

I thought, *awkward!* again, and said, "Um, sure," again and started straightening up the brochures on the rack beside the register.

Miles said, "So what's up?"

What's up? I never know how to answer that. The sky? The national debt?

I said, "Not much." Big improvement over "Um, sure," I know.

Miles said, "Cool."

He came over and stood close beside me. He picked up one of the flyers for a race. It was glossier than the others, which were mostly single-page Xeroxes announcing a 5K, a 10K.

He waved the flyer at me and said, "Can't wait for this."

I looked at it for the first time. He moved closer so I could read it—and when I did, I could hardly breathe. It was for a half marathon in June in a town about ninety miles away.

"There's money," Miles said.

"What do you mean?"

"Cash awards for the top ten runners. It usually attracts a fast crowd, sometimes even Kenyans come, so the pace will be blistering. I just want to beat Nikki and Owen."

"You could win money?" I asked. That would be like being a professional runner.

"Nah," he said. "I'm not that fast. But the race will be stacked with talent. It's my best chance for a PR."

"A personal record—'the best race time at a given distance,'" I said, remembering what Joan had told me, and defining it like an SAT word.

"Yep. Joan is writing me a program so I can peak for this race," he said, shaking the flyer again.

"Cool," I said.

He looked down at the paper Joan had given him before she left the store. "Gotta do a long run tomorrow." He paused. He seemed to be thinking about something. He had rolled the race flyer into a tube. Then he tapped me lightly on the shoulder with it.

"I was wondering," he said slowly, more slowly than he usually spoke, "after I'm finished with my workout, I told Harry—"

"—your grandmother," I interrupted, too eager.

"Yeah. I told her that I'd take Potato out for a trot while I warmed down."

We stood there in awkward silence for a while.

Then he said, "You wanna?"

"Wanna what?"

"Come with?"

I'm sure he must have been able to see my soon-to-expire telltale heart thump-thump-thumping through my shirt. Or heard it drub-drub-drubbing.

I said, "Um, okay."

"Cool," he said. "Meet on the boulevard and Ruffner, around noon?"

"Okay," I said, and immediately worried I wouldn't be able to keep up with him. As if he'd read my mind he said, "It'll be slow. I'll be pretty beat at that point."

"Okay," I said.

He turned to leave. "High noon."

"Okay," I said, pretending to draw a revolver from a holster on my hip and waving it in his direction.

18

I was at home with Walter, telling him how stupid I sounded whenever I was around Miles. I couldn't form a coherent sentence, let alone speak in more than one syllable. I could practically hear Walter saying, "Use your words, Alice."

Instead, he just crunched on a piece of dry macaroni. He makes the funniest, cutest noise when he eats uncooked noodles. You can't believe chewing could be so loud. And so cute.

Maybe he did need some fattening up. So I made him a special treat: a bowl filled with pasta, peanut butter, and the head of a marshmallow Peep. Walter loves him some Peeps. But only the yellow chicks, since they are the best, as we know.

Walter had one leg stretched out taut and was grabbing it with his hands. He looked like a ballet dancer doing exercises. Or like he was playing the cello. That rat had a lot of smooth moves. Sometimes, when he was feeling perky, he would jump into the air straight up, for no reason except to celebrate the joy of having a physical body. And when he wanted to run, oh man, the guy could move.

When he was hard asleep, he'd close his eyes. Often during his naps he would keep them slightly open. He was always aware of his environment. Not worried, but alert to possibilities.

My pied beauty was both predator and prey. He liked to chase my finger or a piece of yarn and I'd call him a predatory panther. But when he snoozed on his back, his feet stuck up in the air and his hands on his chest, he looked as defenseless and vulnerable as a baby. How easy it would be for someone to come and snarf him up.

While he was generally quick to right himself after a back-sleeping session, seeing him so exposed, so trusting, nearly always made me want to cry. He was prepared to take action if necessary, but he lived as if nothing bad would ever happen to him. He knew I would take care of him, that we two together were something formidable and mighty.

Without each other, we'd each be diminished.

And without Jenni, I felt less than myself. We'd never gone this long without talking. But after she'd left the night of my mom's birthday I got mad that she had got mad at me and decided not to call her. It seemed like she'd decided the same thing. We were in a standoff. It made me sad and cranky.

Settling down to read was impossible. I played Snood but felt *restive* ("unable to keep still"). I checked Web sites for the colleges to see if they might have updates on when decisions would be announced, but no. Probably just as well, since I knew what the answers would be. No, no, no, and no. And then more no's.

Walter picked at the Peep, but didn't seem hungry, and also didn't do what he'd normally do, which was take everything I offered and stash it under the bed. He was probably as tired as I was, so I scooped him up, kissed him on the nose, put him back in his cage, and went downstairs, where my parents and Walter-the-Man were watching a Duke basketball game.

I knew they were watching a game because the screams penetrated through the second floor, through Mom's office, through the guest room and the guest bathroom and the guest TV room; the screams crept up through my parents' bedroom and their bathroom; they reverberated through Mom's shoe temple, and through their sitting room, where Dad sometimes huddled with his laptop and watched CNN as if it was porn, and finally they made their way up to me, to my room.

So annoying.

I went downstairs to find a rerun of a scene I'd seen a zillion times before: Mom clenching a magazine, her glasses perched low on her nose as she watched the TV, Dad white-knuckled and mostly silent, and Walter-the-Man shrieking his freaking head off.

Three minutes and forty-seven seconds remained in the first half. The camera alternated between showing the court and zooming in on the genius college students who painted themselves blue and camped out for tickets to the games.

Walter-the-Man: "Three minutes. That's a lot of time. Come on, Duke, you can do it. C'mon, Duke."

Mom: "That little point guard is really holding his own."

Walter-the-Man: [Colorful questioning of the ref's manhood.]

Walter-the-Man: "Yes, oh yes! YES." [Arms raised in the air like an Olympic gymnast sticking a landing.]

Mom: "Nicely done."

Walter-the-Man: "NOOOO! How could you miss a layup like that? *Oy vey* Maria!"

Dad: "*Oy vey* Maria?"

Walter-the-Man: "Nice play, boys, nice play—oh no, not a three. NOT A THREE! Why do they keep trying for all these threes? You know what I always say." [Looks around, first at my dad, who doesn't acknowledge him, and then at my mom, magazine still hanging off her hand, and finally at me, like I care.] "Live by the three, die by the three."

Walter-the-Man: "ARE YOU KIDDING ME? ARE YOU GODDAMN FREAKING KIDDING ME? Is there a lid on that bucket? Does anyone here see a lid on that bucket?" [Looks around to see if anyone sees a lid on that bucket.]

Mom: "This is a better game than I expected. Carolina's been so weak this season."

Walter-the-Man: "Guard your man, you scrawny doofus." [Head in his hands.]

Walter-the-Man: "YES! YES! DE-NIED! DEEEEE-NIED!" [Furious hand-clapping.]

Walter-the-Man: [Cheering along with the blue-painted students on TV.] *"Go to hell, Carolina, go to hell!* [Clap clap.] *Go to hell, Carolina, go to hell!* [Clap clap.]

The buzzer sounded and Mom went back to *Real Simple.* Dad took out his iPad and started on a new crossword. Walter-the-Man shook his empty beer bottle at me.

I shook my head at him.

Me: "Walter-the-Man, did you go to Duke?"

Walter-the-Man: "No, Alice, I did not."

Me: "Do you have any actual connection to Duke?"

Walter-the-Man: [Slowly.] "No. I do not."

Me: "So both of my parents have graduate degrees from Duke. I can sort of understand why they would spend their time watching this team. But you are crazy for Duke and have no connection to the school. Don't you think that's strange? Most people around here root for U. Or Kentucky. Why Duke?"

Mom: "Alice."

Me: "Well, isn't it a little weird to be so fanatical about a team you have no real link to?"

There's a car commercial and another car commercial, and then these two commentators start talking about the game.

Me: "Did you ever play college basketball?"

Dad: [Warning look.]

Walter-the-Man: "No, Alice, I didn't."

Me: "High school?"

Mom: [Sharply.] "Alice."

I knew I should shut up and go back to my room. When

I got in a pissy mood like this, I knew I should avoid humans. But the whole thing made no sense to me. Walter-the-Man planned his life around Duke basketball games. Most of them he watched at our house, whether or not my parents were home. He came in, got himself a beer from the fridge, and settled on the couch for two hours of screaming at the television.

Me: "I mean, really. Don't you have more important things to do?"

Walter-the-Man: [Looks down at his empty beer bottle. He picks at the edge of the label. He crosses one leg over the other, uncrosses it, and looks right at me. He leans forward.]

Walter-the-Man: "Hmmm. Let me think. Do I have more important things to do? Like what? Like make tons of money defending multinational corporations that do indefensible things? Right. I already do that. I spend most of my waking hours doing that.

"The fact is, Alice, I love being a fan. I am, in fact, the very definition of a fan, 'a fanatic,' especially when it comes to Duke basketball. When I see these kids play, when I watch a team come together and become something bigger than each individual man, when I see a beautiful play, a buzzer-beating shot—where everything goes right, everything is in sync, when the impossible happens—it makes me believe. Not in God or anything spiritual—I stopped believing in God when I quit being an altar boy, but in possibility. It makes me feel part of something special. I met your father in a bar because we were both watching Duke play and we discovered we worked for the same firm, and we both said it was something we'd do only for a while because it was soul-sucking, life-deadening work. But here we both still are. Your father has your mother and you, which is a good thing when you're not being a pain in the ass. [He winks. Like a skeevy old man. He actually winks.]

"Me? Watching this team each season makes me come alive in a way that, you may find this hard to believe, corporate law does not. It helps me forget—though your mother is nice enough to remind me—that I'm fifty years old and still dating. It makes me forget my receding hairline and my increasing waist size. I have no family, no kids, I don't even have a dog or a plant, but what I do have is a couple of handfuls of young men whose physical talents impress the bejesus out of me and whose stories I get to know because they inspire and delight me.

"I could never jump that high, or run that fast, or handle a ball with such grace. When I follow this team I become invested in something outside myself. I care. And this is what I know: not caring is the end of a meaningful life. To be cynical about everything is a sad way to live. I don't want to doubt; I want to believe. I want to feel passionate about something. I love it when Duke wins. I want them to go all the way to the big dance, the Final Four. I want them to win another national championship like you would not believe.

"But even when they lose, while I'm not happy, I'm kind of happy I'm not happy. You know what I mean? I mean, it feels good to feel something. And it's something I can share with other people.

"I can walk into any bar and have a conversation with the guy—or the woman—on the next stool, where all of the things that make us different fall away and we can talk for hours about this game, or last season, or players long since retired, and it doesn't matter if I'm a sad sack of a lawyer and he's a housepainter who married his high school sweetheart and never went to college, or if she voted for people I think are evil, because that stuff never comes up.

"We are citizens of the nation of basketball and for a few minutes, or an hour, or the length of the game, for that brief amount of time, I feel less alone in the world."

[He gets up and walks to the kitchen for another beer.]

19

I couldn't sleep that night.

When I wasn't worrying about my run with Miles, I was wondering what Jenni was doing and if she was going to call me, or thinking about what Walter-the-Man had said about being passionate. I couldn't come up with anything I cared about as much as Walter-the-Man cared about Duke basketball.

I ate breakfast early because I didn't want to get a cramp when I was running with Miles, and I took a shower and washed my hair. Yes, I washed my hair before I went for a run. I even used some mascara. For a minute I wished that Jenni was there to help me, but then I remembered I was mad at her.

I put on my running clothes and waited. I didn't know how I was going to last until noon.

Walter was sleeping and didn't want to come out of his cage. So I left him in there and played some rounds of Freerice until I kept getting *pulchritude* wrong. There's no way such a hideous word should mean "physically attractive."

After about a hundred hours it got to be quarter to twelve. I jogged to the boulevard and could see, waiting for me at the corner, Miles and Potato.

Don't sound stupid, I told myself.

Be yourself, I self–pep talked.

And then I thought, God no! Don't be yourself. That will scare him off.

"Hey," Miles said when he saw me. He wore short black shorts and a black shirt with a blocky picture of a guy running and the words *Pre Lives.*

"Hey," I said, and then Potato was on me. He danced on his itsy back legs and hit my knees with his front feet. His toenails were long black talons. He wagged his tail so hard his whole body vibrated. I bent down and he jumped up and planted a wet one on my nose. Today he sported a leopard-print harness.

"He likes you," Miles said.

I sat on the sidewalk and Potato crawled into my lap. He kept putting his head against me and waiting to be petted. I cooed to him the way I do to Walter, saying things like, "You sweet little man, you munchkin poochie."

Don't be yourself! I remembered, too late.

I stood up and brushed the paw prints off my tights. "He's nice," I said, trying to be cool.

"You an animal person?" Miles asked.

"Yeah, I guess," I said. I realized I didn't want to tell him about Walter because of the whole kids-with-rats-are-loner-weirdos thing.

"Spud," Miles said suddenly, "run?" Potato stood at alert, his ears pricked as high as they could go, which, like the rest of him, was not very. His tail stood straight up. "Wanna?" Miles said, and Potato wagged like a maniac.

"Wanna?" he said to me.

And we started.

20

At first all I could think about was how hard I was breathing. You could probably hear me two counties away.

Miles said, "Need to take it easy," and was running—jogging—so slowly I couldn't believe it.

After a few minutes, I felt like I could go that speed all day. I relaxed. Then Miles started talking and I stopped paying attention to what was going on in my body and just listened to him.

His grandmother had forced him to watch a movie the night before. It was one of her favorites, she said, and he simply had to watch it with her. He said it exactly like this and I giggled.

"What's funny?" he asked.

"Uh, nothing. It's just kind of cute the way you said you 'simply had to watch it with her.'"

"Huh. Guess it's just a phrase she uses a lot."

He told me how he stayed at her house on weekend nights and they had a routine. His grandfather had died a long time ago and Harry had never remarried. She occasionally had "friends" over, but she'd lived alone for a long time. She was, he said, fun to hang out with. I thought it was sweet he liked to spend time with his grandmother. Then I realized she was no ordinary grandma.

For movie-night dinners Harry made two gigantic bowls of popcorn—one for each of them—and hot chocolate, prepared with Mexican chocolate and a splash of hazelnut liqueur. She doctored the popcorn with a combination of flaxseed oil and olive oil and sprinkled a hefty dose of brewer's yeast on it.

"Whatever flaxseed oil and brewer's yeast are, that sounds disgusting."

"Harry claims they're the secrets to her health."

"That, and the liqueur," I added. He laughed.

Last night's movie was *Harold and Maude*, he said, a romance between a teenage boy and a seventy-nine-year-old woman.

"Sounds great," I said, being sarcastic, and then worrying that he would think I was bitchy.

"It was," Miles said. "Totally freaking awesome."

But the more he told me about it, the more bizarre it seemed. The boy, Harold, was obsessed with death and dying. And then he met Maude, who loved life more than anyone. Maude reminded Miles of Harry.

"You should see it," Miles said. "And the sound track is great. It's by Cat Stevens."

My mother listened to Cat Stevens once in a while. When I was little, she used to sing "Moonshadow" to me, especially when I followed her around the house.

"Maybe I will."

"What's your favorite movie?" he asked me.

That was easy. *"Ratatouille."*

"That kids' cartoon about the rat?"

I tried not to hear judgment in his voice.

"Yes," I said.

"Hard to imagine a rat being a sympathetic character, much less a hero."

I said nothing. I was glad I hadn't mentioned Walter to him.

We ran in silence for a while and then Miles asked, "So what do you like about it?

"Besides everything?"

"Including everything."

"Well," I said, and started in. "What I love most is the message: anyone can cook but only the fearless can be great. I love the idea that cooking—and cooking, of course, stands in for most things in life—is something anyone can do with enough effort. But there are those who are, well, talented in ways others aren't. Our generation has been fed this diet of 'You are all beautiful and unique snow-flakes.' I think that's hooey. Some snowflakes are better than others. But we're not supposed to say that. The idea that someone can find his or her talent—and passion— and pursue it to the nth degree is something I envy. Last night Walter-the-M—"

I stopped myself because I realized, maybe for the first time, that it was strange I called him Walter-the-Man, and if I explained that, I'd have to explain about Walter.

"—um, a family friend, was talking about how much he loves being a Duke basketball fan. I didn't get it before, how having a passion can help you to live. But that's exactly what *Ratatouille* is about. Remy is the kid who doesn't fit in because he likes something other people don't understand. Well, other rats. You know what I mean." I was getting flustered because I knew I could sound all nerdy when I talked like this. But I couldn't stop.

"He gets an opportunity to follow his passion and it takes him places. That movie makes me think if I could only figure out what I'm interested in, I could excel at something. And I like the idea that while not everyone can become a great artist, a great artist can come from anywhere."

Miles ran beside me and listened. I was talking fast and was already breathless from running.

But I kept going. "Plus, there are all these other things about the movie I love. I love that when he gets swept away in the water, Remy is saved by a book. The book literally is his life raft. I often think books help me to live."

I was all excited because I was figuring out more as I was speaking. Sometimes I don't really know what I think until I talk or write about it. "Plus, I like the point the movie makes about how, in a good book, the author comes to life. You feel like he's talking to you, directly to you, answering your questions and thinking your thoughts, even though that seems nutty. Good books feel personal. Even, I guess, cookbooks. Reading is a cure for loneliness."

"Yeah," Miles said. "I know something about that, being an only child who lives in the sticks."

"Plus," I said, because I really couldn't stop now, "I love

how much I learned about food and cooking. I like books and movies where I get to learn stuff in a way that feels fun. I don't like to cook or bake but I like knowing you can tell a good bread by the sound the crust makes. I like to know you have to have a 'clean station' when you're working in the kitchen."

We were running faster now, and I think it was because of me. I was fired up. "Plus, it's beautiful. I mean, it's a piece of art. The movie is art and the food they show in the movie is art."

I also wanted to say that they got the rat movements exactly right. The way rats run and jump and leap. The way they stand on their back feet and are able to lean forward at an angle without falling over—it was clear to me that the animators had spent time with actual rats. But I didn't mention any of that.

While I felt ashamed about betraying Walter by thinking of him as something embarrassing, I was afraid Miles wouldn't understand.

21

After I finished babbling on, Miles was quiet for a while. I worried that now he would definitely think I was the freak of all freaks, but then he said he felt the same way about running—that there are so many things about it that he loves, and that in some ways, a race can be like a work of art. He quoted this guy named Steve Prefontaine— "Pre"—a track star back in the '70s who said something like, "I don't race to find out who's the fastest. I race to find out who has the most guts."

I'd never thought of running like that, about the need to be fearless. I remembered what the winner of the Red Dress Run had said about Joan, that she didn't have the guts. I asked Miles what that was all about.

"The trials," he said. "Thirteen years ago."

"Was she arrested?" I couldn't imagine Joan doing anything that even stretched the law.

He made a playful jab at my shoulder. "No, dude, the Olympic trials. For the marathon. It's the race before the Olympics that determines who gets to represent the U.S."

"A marathon before the marathon?"

"Yeah, it's held about six months before the games.

First three in the race earn their Olympic berths, so you're racing for position, rather than time. That's kind of what did Joan in."

It was like we weren't even running, just chatting like normal people. While we were running! Not having to look at him actually made it easier to talk. Potato cruised along and then he stopped short.

He'd found a tree he had to pee on.

We waited for him to put his leg back down and then started floating along again.

"Joan went into the trials with the fastest qualifying time that year. She was a lock for the team. But she didn't go for it. She played it safe and stayed with the lead pack. Barely held on for fourth place, which, in the trials, is as good—or as bad—as last. People thought she had wimped out, said she didn't have the guts to run by herself."

"Is that what you think?"

He was quiet for a while. We listened to each other's breathing. Or more likely, he listened to me panting.

Finally he said, "Yeah, I guess. It seems like a gigantic washout. She never raced again."

Failure seemed to be the theme of my life right now. Not something I wanted to discuss, so instead I said, "This is a long run for me."

"You have a nice easy stride," Miles said, looking me up and down. "And good form."

I got all embarrassed and said, "Tell me what I'm doing wrong."

"Nothing. Not a thing."

"No," I said, too loud. "Help me."

"You don't need help. You're doing great."

"You know there's always something that could be better. I hate not being good at things."

"You're just beginning. You don't have to be good yet. You just have to keep at it. Build your strength, increase your endurance, and eventually get around to adding some speed."

"Tell me something that will help."

He sighed. "Maybe try to relax your shoulders, and don't clench your fists."

I had rolled my fingers into a tight ball.

"Shake out your hands," he said, and acted like he was trying to get the blood back into the tips of his digits. "When you're running, pretend you're holding two fistfuls of potato chips."

When he said "potato," the little guy turned around and looked at him. "Excuse me. Chips. Pretend you have chips in your hands. You don't want to crush them."

"What else?"

"Well," he said, drawing the word out. "Don't swing your arms past the midpoint of your body. If you think about rotating your thumbs out, that can help."

"Okay," I said, and thought about my imaginary potato chip–filled hands with the thumbs turned out. I might have looked like a hitchhiker with arthritis. "What else?"

"If you want to speed up, shorten your stride."

"Take smaller steps?"

"Yep. It'll increase your turnover."

"Okay. Good. What else?"

Miles laughed and said, "Look. Running is the most natural thing in the world. It's the act of catching yourself before you fall. If you pitch your upper body forward, your leg will shoot out. Can't help it. Sometimes you might fall. I go down all the time on the trails. But you brush yourself off and keep going. Running is just a controlled fall. Kind of like life."

"Deep," I said.

"I know, right?" he said.

"Seriously. Thank you," I said.

Then he did something crazy. He put a finger against one nostril and blew a wad of snot out of his nose.

"WTF?" I said.

"Snot rocket," he said.

That might have been more than I needed to know. I remembered seeing the book in his backpack at the race.

"So do you like to read?" I said like a gigantic nerd.

"Read all the time," he said. "Right now I'm digging *The Things They Carried*."

"Really? I love that book so much."

He nodded, as if there could be no other response, and continued. "My all-time fave, though, is *Catcher in the Rye*."

"No way," I said.

"Kind of cliché to love it, right?"

"Are you kidding me? I hate it. Hate it. Hate it."

He didn't do that thing people sometimes do when I express a strong opinion—or express the same opinion three times—and say, "Why don't you tell us how you really feel?" I hate when people say that. Why would we be having a conversation if I wasn't going to tell you how I really feel?

Instead, he said, "Huh," and guided us across the street.

We were almost back to where we'd started. On the way out, we had run by a youngish couple sitting on a porch and yelling at each other. They were still there, but now they were making out like crazy. Miles must have noticed it too, because he looked at me and grinned.

"You must be tired," I said, feeling uncomfortable for some reason. "How far did you go today total?"

"Around seventeen," he said. "I'm a little beat," he added, although there was no way to tell. When he ran he didn't make a sound. It was as if his feet stayed above the ground like one of those hovercrafts they used to cross the English Channel. You could hear my feet hit. Every. Single. Step.

"How far have we gone?"

"At the corner it will be five miles."

"*Five miles!* I've never run that far before."

"Now you have. Easy, right?"

"Easier than I could have imagined."

"You're a natural. Before long, you'll be busting out a half marathon."

"Don't think so," I said, but I wondered: Could I do a half marathon? That would be something to aim for. That would be an achievement.

Potato had started to lag behind. I thought maybe he

was trying to save face by pretending to be a big man, peeing on things when what he needed was to take a break. Maybe I was just projecting.

"This was fun," I said, when we got back to Ruffner.

Miles stood on the curb with his heel hanging over, stretching first one long lean leg and then the other.

I pondered the things I'd learned about him in addition to his questionable choice in favorite books: his dad was a carpenter and his mom baked bread and supplied local restaurants. His parents had a big organic garden and they sold vegetables at the farmers' market in the summer. I didn't tell him I'd written my personal statement about how much I hated Holden Caulfield. I'd been able to skip over the whole college-admissions thing because Miles didn't seem to care about college at all. He said when he was finished with high school, which would be next January, he thought he'd probably go woofing.

I said, "Is this something to do with Potato?"

He laughed and spelled it out: WWOOF, World Wide Opportunities on Organic Farms. It was a global network where you could volunteer to work on different farms.

"Lots of people take a gap year between high school and college—or during college, or even when they're adults on vacation—to become WWOOFers. You can do beekeeping in Italy, be a shepherd in New Zealand, pick Syrah grapes in France, harvest coffee beans in Kenya. You get room and board in exchange for work. Harry thinks I need to see more of the world, and this would be one way to do it."

"Wow," I said. And I barked out, "Woof."

Then I barked some more. "Woof woof woof!"

Potato cocked his head at me as if I was crazy, and I may have been. It had never occurred to me you could do anything other than go straight to college.

Then Miles said, "Woof." And Potato shook his head so that the tags on his collar tinkled like the beginning of a song.

22

When I got back to the house, my mother said, "You were gone a long time. Is everything okay?"

"Now you're timing my runs? What's next? Measuring how fast my hair grows?"

"Excuse me for worrying about you," she said, and if she could have frowned, she would have been frowning big-time.

"Don't worry about me."

"Fine," she said.

"Fine," I said.

Then I felt bad and said, "It's just that I'm getting better at running and have been able to go longer."

I didn't want to tell her about Miles. It would make her too happy. She's always saying I need more friends, and aren't there any cute guys at school?

She said, "Have you spoken to Jenni?"

I didn't answer, just went into the kitchen and poured myself a big glass of chocolate milk. I took it into the living room and lay down on the floor and smiled to myself thinking about how Miles and I had ended the run woofing

at each other. I realized we still hadn't exchanged numbers and wondered when I'd see him again.

I tried to do some stretching. Unsuccessful. Then I ended
up falling asleep. I'm sure I still had a smile on my face.

I woke up starving, so I went into the kitchen and
made myself a pb&j-with-banana sandwich to share with
the dude upstairs.

Walter was in his cage, hunched and trembling. His fur
was sticking up and he looked disheveled.

When I opened his door, he didn't move.

"What's the matter, little man?" I put my hand in, and
normally he would have run over to it.

But he didn't.

He stayed hunched and trembling.

"Walter. Walter?"

He looked skinny. And frail. And there was something
red around his nose and eyes. It looked like blood. Oh god,
it looked like blood.

Gently I grabbed him and pulled him out. He didn't
look at me.

I put him on my pillow and he continued to shake. I ran
downstairs and called out for my mom.

"Mom!"

She didn't answer.

"Mommy!"

I found her in the living room.

"Something's wrong with Walter."

23

I put the travel cage on the floor of the car but held Walter in my hands. His whole body was shuddering and his eyes were closed.

Mom had called ahead and said the vet would see us when we got there. She looked at Walter and said, "Sweet little guy."

Mom had come a long way to be able to say that.

I had been asking for a dog for forever, and finally, on my fourteenth birthday, Mom said, "Alice. No dogs. You can have a small pet that will stay in your room. A hamster, maybe. A guinea pig. But no dogs. I don't have the time to do all the work a dog would require."

So we went to the pet store, and, while I was tempted by the mice, when I saw Walter and his brothers, I knew that was it.

"Come on, Alice," my mother said, like I was being annoying, like I wanted a rat just to upset her.

"What's wrong with a rat?"

"Why can't you get a hamster? Or a gerbil?"

And that was that. The more she tried to convince me

not to get a rat, the more I knew a rat was the perfect pet for me.

The pet store guy opened the top of the rat cage and asked which one I wanted.

How to pick? I had no idea.

"What about this fellow?" He plucked one of them out by his tail and put him on the flat of his hand. The rat immediately pooped out four good-size pellets. Mom groaned.

"Not him," I said.

He picked up another one, who cowered in his hand.

"Nope."

Then he picked up Walter. Instead of seeming scared, Walter was curious. He nosed the guy's hand and sat up on his hind legs and sniffed the air. He looked at me.

"Can I pet him?"

"Sure," said the guy. "The rats never bite. The hamsters, those little bastards—um, those suckers, will draw blood. The gerbils too, if they get scared. But the rats, never."

I held my finger out so Walter could smell it. He grabbed it with his tiny star hands and put it in his mouth. I pulled away.

"He's not going to bite you—he's exploring."

So I gave him back my finger and he didn't bite. Instead, he nibbled under my nail. My first manicure from him.

"This one," I said. "This one."

We got his cage, and to line it the guy recommended something that came in a bunch of colors and looked like shredded egg cartons or clumped-up toilet paper—not wood shavings, the pet store guy said. Cedar and pine give off acids toxic to rats. My mother made me promise to clean the cage at least once a week. *No problemo,* I said.

We got him pellets of food, some wooden chew toys shaped like vegetables, and a wheel to run on. He ran on the wheel exactly once. Did a few laps and that was the end of it for him. I can imagine that is the way I would feel about running on a treadmill.

24

When we got to the vet's office, they showed us into a room. I held Walter—he wanted to be near my neck—and Mom carried the cage. The vet, a large woman with short gray hair, came in and said, "Let's see what's going on with this cutie."

She reached for him.

Walter, who usually loves new people, didn't even look up. Just let her take him.

She looked at his eyes and nose, used a stethoscope to listen to his heart.

"He's an old-timer," she said.

Mom nodded.

I thought, What?

"How long have you had him?"

"It will be four years on my birthday, in a couple of months."

She made a low sound, an *I see* sound. "How big was he when you got him?"

"About that size," I said. I didn't know exactly how old Walter was, so we always celebrated my birthday and his adoption day, which were the same.

"That's ancient for a rat. They generally only live a thousand days."

A thousand days?

I couldn't do the math. If Walter was four years old, how many days was that? Walter was old?

"He's in pain. That's why he's hunched over and why his hair is sticking up. This red stuff around his eyes and nose isn't blood, it's porphyrin. It's an indication of stress. Has he been eating?"

I shook my head.

No. No. No.

How had I not noticed he'd gotten so old? He looked the same as he always did—until I saw him in the vet's hands. Saw how skinny he was, how his fur wasn't sleek and glossy the way it had been. He'd been moving slowly, jumping less, sleeping more. I had been so focused on my college applications and on running and on Miles I hadn't been paying enough attention.

Mom put her hand on my shoulder and I shook it off.

The vet said, "It looks like he's led a good and healthy life. We don't usually see rats this old. As you know, rats do everything fast. Including completing their life span. He's lived far beyond what you could expect. Obviously you've taken great care of him."

This couldn't be happening.

This could not be happening.

I took Walter from the vet and sat down. I held him up to my face and kissed him. Normally he would raise a front paw and push me away. Or he'd kiss me back on the lips. Now he stayed hunched.

He wouldn't look up.

The vet and my mother were whispering. Mom came and sat next to me. She tried to put her arm around me. I moved away.

The vet crouched down to talk to me. She said, "We can give him some pain medication, but he doesn't have much time left."

Mom said, "Alice, the hardest thing in the world is to watch someone you love suffer."

I shook my head. This could not be happening.

He was fine.

He had to be fine.

Mom said, "With people, we do everything we can to prolong their lives, even when what it means to be alive seems far worse than the alternative. Human medicine hasn't caught up to this." She gestured to the room, to the vet. "People don't get to make the choice when they've had enough. We keep pumping them with chemicals and putting them through tests, doping them into oblivion. They never get to say, 'Enough. I'm ready.'"

"But I'm not ready. I thought, I thought—"

I thought he was going to live forever. That I'd be taking him to college with me next year. That I'd be living with him when I'd finished college and was out in the world working. Even though I knew that wasn't reasonable, I could never force myself to imagine him dying.

"Honey," she said, smoothing my hair, "I know. We're

never ready. You need to decide what's right for Walter. If you think it's best, we can take him home and try to keep him comfortable with pain meds."

"Oh my little dude," I said, and petted his head. He didn't move. His eyes were squinty. He was shaking. "I love you so much."

I couldn't stand to see him in pain, and I couldn't stand to be without him.

"Leave me alone with him," I said. "Please."

The vet took my mom's arm and they walked out of the room.

As soon as they were gone I went cold. The room smelled scary, like a hospital. Walter trembled in my hands. I told him how sorry I was. I should have known. I should have realized. In all my rat research, in all my Googling of things related to rodents, I had always skipped over anything that mentioned how long they lived. Even when people asked, which they sometimes did, I just said I didn't know and why would they focus on something so morbid?

I held him up to my neck and, with what seemed like a lot of effort, he nestled his head under my chin.

We stayed like that for a long time.

25

Pied Beauty

Glory be to God for dappled things—
　　For skies of couple-colour as a brinded cow;
　　　For rose-moles all in stipple upon trout
　　　　that swim;
Fresh-firecoal chestnut-falls; finches' wings;
　　Landscape plotted and pieced—fold, fallow,
　　　and plough;
　　　And áll trádes, their gear and tackle and
　　　　trim.

All things counter, original, spare, strange;
　　Whatever is fickle, freckled (who knows
　　　how?)
　　　With swift, slow; sweet, sour; adazzle,
　　　　dim;
He fathers-forth whose beauty is past change:
　　　　Praise him.

—Gerard Manley Hopkins

PART
THREE

Woke up.
   Didn't get out of bed.
   Didn't eat.
   Didn't run.
   Didn't go to school.
   Didn't read.
   Didn't play Snood.
   Didn't get dressed.
   Didn't wash my face.
   Didn't want to live.

2

I slept in the second-floor guest room because I couldn't stand to be in my room.

I couldn't stop searching the floor for him, couldn't keep my eyes away from where he used to be.

When Dorothy wakes up back in Kansas, all the Technicolor is gone. She's back to a sepia-toned life with Auntie Em and a bunch of farmhands.

But at least she still has Toto.

I had no color left.

Mom and Dad asked what I wanted to do with Walter's cage and I told them to get rid of it.

3

How could I have been so stupid?

How had I not noticed he was getting old and sick?

How was it possible, with everything I'd learned about rats, that I didn't know how long they were expected to live?

How could I have missed something this big?

4

My parents let me take a few days off from school but then I had to go back.

I walked with my head down so no one could see that I was crying pretty much all the time. I hid out in the library during lunch.

In class I let Sam Malouf ramble on without contradicting the stupid things he said.

I wrote Walter's name over and over in my notebook.

Jenni had left me a million texts and e-mails, which I didn't read before I deleted them.

I silenced my phone after the third time she called.

5

REJECTED:
Yale
Harvard
Princeton
Cornell
Brown
Emory
Vanderbilt
Middlebury

ADMITTED:
Trinity
Bowdoin

FUTURE:
Uncertain

6

When I heard the knock on the guest-room door, I said, "Go away."

"Al," Jenni said, "can I come in?"

"No. Go away." I added, "Please." We hadn't spoken to or seen each other since the horrible birthday debacle the previous week. I knew she'd been in the house, knew she'd been talking to my mother.

I heard her slump against the other side of the door.

"I know how much you're hurting."

I started to say, "No, you don't," but then I thought about how she'd crumpled in the days after her mother died. We were just kids, but I remembered thinking that was when she had suddenly gotten older than me.

"Al," Jenni said through the door. "He had a great life. No rat—maybe no one—has ever been more loved than Walter. You were his world, and it was a great world. At least he got to be old."

I suspected she was thinking of her mom, who died so young.

Nothing she could say was going to make me feel better. Nothing.

I wanted her to stop talking about him.

I said, "You can come in."

When she opened the door, I saw she was carrying a bowl of Easy Mac and a diet A&W root beer. As soon as I smelled the cheesy goodness of the Easy Mac, I felt hungry.

I reached out for it, and when I remembered it was one of Walter's favorite foods, I started to cry.

She sat next to me on the bed. I couldn't control my body. It shook with sobs that erupted from deep inside. It didn't take long for Jenni to start crying and we held each other and cried and cried and cried.

After a while, I started getting a headache and said that we were going to get dehydrated.

Jenni said, "I was afraid we were going to be swept away in a pool of Alice tears."

I surprised myself—and Jenni—by laughing.

Then Jenni laughed.

And then both of us were both laughing and crying.

7

When I made it into work it was clear that *someone* had tipped Joan off. She said, "I understand you lost a friend."

I nodded.

"Let me know if there's anything I can do to help," she said, and drew me into one of her tight hugs.

And that was it. She didn't try to give me advice or tell me what I could expect to feel. She didn't say she was sorry, or that he was only a rat. She held me close and when she let go she swatted my back and said, "We got a big shipment in and I've been hopeless in trying to get things organized. You know me," she added with a shrug and a smile.

As I moved toward the stockroom Joan said, "Miles has been asking about you. Said he hasn't seen you on the boulevard."

I said nothing.

Miles was the last person I wanted to see. I didn't want to have to explain that my world had collapsed because someone he didn't think could be a sympathetic character had died.

"Not running?"

I shook my head and went toward the messy pile of boxes.

After a couple of hours sorting through new pairs of shoes, checking them off in the computer inventory, getting price tags on three boxes of new shorts and shirts, I emerged from the stockroom just before closing time. Joan was tidying up the START wall.

I didn't know what to say and I didn't really want to go home yet, so I asked the question I'd been wondering about.

"Do you have a number up there?"

"Sure do," she said, and pointed to a race bib way up in the corner. The number was 1. Across the top it said: *U.S. Olympic Trials.*

"My last race as a competitive runner. The most important day of my life. That race made me who I am today."

Could she be referring to the same race Miles had told me about? The day she failed?

"It's funny. I haven't thought about it for a long time. I don't know if you know anything about my running history." She looked at me and grinned. "I used to be a fairly good runner."

"Yeah, I'd heard that."

She turned back to the wall. "I'm sure you did," she said with a soft chuckle.

Then she put her hands on her hips and looked back at me.

"Hey, since we're about to close, do you want to go out for a little jog?"

Even if I had been running every day—which I hadn't—I certainly wasn't fast enough to run with Joan. As I started to say no she said, "It'll be slow and easy. And I'll tell you about the trials and what happened after."

I wanted to hear, but wasn't sure I wanted to run.

"Come on," she said. "Let's do it. There are some stories that are better told while moving forward."

So we did what we needed to close up the store. I swept and vacuumed and emptied the trash and Joan put the cash from the register in the safe. She'd encouraged me to keep an extra set of running clothes and shoes in the stockroom for those times when, as she said, "You just have to go for a run." After we'd both changed clothes, she flipped over the sign on the door that said GONE RUNNING, and we headed out.

Joan took short, quick steps. It was beautiful to see her legs in motion; she moved like a ballet dancer. I was able to notice because I hung back and ran behind her for the first block. She turned, jogging backward, and said, "Come on, Alice. I know you can keep up."

I didn't know that I could.

By the time I got to her I was panting. She just kept going, her arms at right angles to her body, her movements efficient and smooth.

Daylight saving time had started the week before and it was still light out, would be for another hour and a half or so. The air felt heavy but not too cold.

We ran without speaking for a while and then Joan said, "I went into the trials that year with the fastest time. I always had the fastest times. I was perhaps the most competitive person you've ever met."

I snorted, because my mother was the most competitive person I'd ever met.

Joan continued. "I'd been racing for a long time, and I always raced to win. Usually I did. I spent hours— sometimes days and nights—before a race throwing up. My whole identity was wrapped around my times, my trophies, my wins. I'd get so hyped up I was barely human. I yelled at everyone, including Ricardo, the man I'd later marry. I knew once I stepped up to the marathon, I had to go to the Olympic Games. It was what I wanted more than anything."

It felt strange to be running again. I'd not gone since Walter died and it was like my body had forgotten how. I tried to imitate Joan's short stride and found that when I did, I went faster and it was easier. Miles had been right.

When we got to a traffic light, I kept jogging in place because I thought you were supposed to—I'd seen people doing it. Joan stood still while we waited for the light to change, so I felt embarrassed and stopped my calisthenics.

When the green man signaled GO, we ran across the street.

Joan went on. "All I had to do was place in the top three. I knew the other girls, and knew I could beat them. But I also wanted to take it easy and not tax myself. I had been dealing with some nagging injuries and I didn't want to get hurt before the games.

"The pace started out slow. I didn't want to push it, so I

sat on the heels of the lead pack and let them do the work. We ran together in a tight bunch. Some of the girls were chatting, talking easily in the first few miles about this and that. I was focused. I never talked during races."

Then she laughed. "Now you can't get me to shut up on a run."

I oinked out something to let her know I was still listening.

"I kept waiting for someone to make a move, to pick up the pace. No one did. I knew I could go a lot faster, but I didn't want to run by myself and was afraid if I threw in a surge, no one would come with me. It's hard to lead a race. It takes more physical effort and it's mentally fatiguing." Her voice, usually soft, had taken on an edge I'd never heard in it. For the first time, I was able to imagine her as a fierce competitor.

"But the pace was too slow. If you run too far off your natural pace, you'll affect your form. I had to make small adjustments in my stride and ended up with blisters, horrendous blisters, about nineteen miles into the marathon."

As she said this, I thought about the first day I came into the store. She'd warned me about wearing cotton socks because of blisters.

"Uh-oh," I said. "Are you going to get blisters from this?" I gestured outward, meaning running now, here, with me.

She patted me on the shoulder and said, "No. It really only happens in long races. Running with you is a pleasure, Alice."

She thought for a moment and said, "In a way, all races

are about managing pain. I'd always been able to run past the point when most people want to stop. When they put me on a treadmill to measure my blood lactate I got it higher than anyone could believe. I was used to the pain of pushing my body hard. But the blisters—a whole different thing. My stride was messed up and I could feel my socks filling with blood."

"Ick," I said, and then realized that was probably not the right thing to say. But Joan was in her own world. She just kept talking and I kept trying to keep up with her.

"After taking the lead and feeling strong, I had to drop way back because of the blisters. I was able to hold on and finish fourth. I realized how tough I was. Like Miles's hero, Pre, I believed I could take more pain than anyone. I was proud of myself, even though, to the rest of the world, I had failed. And, of course, I had. I broke the most important rule: I didn't run my own race. I waited for the other girls and let them set the pace. I was too scared to go out on my own. I had failed in the most awful, public way. Fourth at the Olympic trials."

Out of the corner of my eye I could see her shaking her head.

"I'd never dropped out of a race before and I didn't that time. I endured. Afterward, I didn't want to talk about it."

She was quiet for a while.

I heard my own breathing and my heavy footfalls. Like Miles, Joan ran without making a sound. I was glad we weren't facing each other. I was afraid of what I would see on her face as she remembered that difficult time.

"Then Ricardo asked me if I still loved running. *Did I love running?* It was what I did. Who I was. Yeah, he said, but do you love it? I realized I took no joy in winning, only vague satisfaction in not losing."

Her hand went to the gold chain around her neck. I'd often seen her fiddle with it at the store, as if she needed to make sure it was still there. "I'd just met Ricardo."

We got to another traffic light and when we stopped she turned toward me. Her eyes were wet but she was smiling. "He loved everything he did; he loved the world. He was happy being outside and didn't care how fast he was moving. When we'd go for a run, he'd want to stop to tell me the names of the flowers and the trees. He'd spot a hawk slicing through the sky overhead, or point out scat from a moose or fox.

"What I had to admit was that I didn't love running anymore, and hadn't for a long time. I was addicted to being good at it. It was like a job I didn't know how to quit, because I didn't know how to do—or be—anything else."

I was so busy listening to her I didn't think about how far we had gone or how fast we were going.

"Ricardo brought me to a playground and made me watch the children dashing around. 'Remember how it feels to run like a kid?' he asked. I didn't. I knew how to train, how to make myself run when the weather was crappy, knew how to do two workouts a day and nap in between. Until I met Ricardo, I'd never slept in on a weekend morning, never lounged around in bed with the Sunday paper and sipped coffee.

"After the trials, everyone thought I quit racing because I had failed. I didn't give any interviews, didn't tell anyone about my blisters or talk about the fact that I had chickened out. Ricardo encouraged me to run with him—at an easy pace—and on those runs he would ask me what I wanted, what I cared about. I hadn't ever thought about anything other than winning. I wanted to learn to love running. I had a natural talent, and I'd taken it as far as it was going to go. I had been able to find out how resilient I was. I could get through the bad spots. What I wanted to recover, and Ricardo helped me do this, was the joy, the delight you see in those kids on the playground."

I snuck a peek at her. She looked lighter, like a kid.

"So we came up with the idea for the store. I wanted to be able to serve the runners who were serious, for whom shaving minutes off a marathon time was a big deal. Ricardo wanted to help people learn to enjoy running. Getting to the start line of the Olympic trials marathon was my big achievement. He said I needed to remember that. I wanted to help others get to the start.

"A couple of weeks after the trials Ricardo gave me this"—she touched the necklace—"and said, 'If you had won gold at the Olympics, you would have taken the medal and locked it away in a safe somewhere. But after the trophies have been awarded, after the times have been posted, what matters is feeling that there is more to come. That you have more to do. You're a link in a chain. Connect to other people and connect them to each other. That will last.'"

After Walter died, I thought I had no more tears left in me.

I was wrong.

Joan said, "I found joy in running, and I found a job that was perfect for me, and I found my partner in life. Even after I lost him—" And she stopped.

She turned and looked at me hard, and by then both of us were silently crying. "—I knew as much as it hurt, and it hurt more than anything I have ever experienced, I would be able to keep going. Running taught me that. Running got me through his illness and his death. It keeps me going still."

8

I studied for the AP exams that were coming up next month because it was easier to "Analyze the cultures of the Mediterranean region during the period circa 200 CE to 1000 CE" or to "Select a single pivotal moment in the psychological or moral development of the protagonist of a bildungsroman and write a well-organized essay that shows how that single moment shapes the meaning of the work as a whole" than it was to think about anything else.

Mom wore the face that said *I'm worried about you*, and she tried to get me to talk about which college I was going to pick. I had until May 1 to make a decision. That didn't leave me much time to decide where I wanted to go.

But the truth was, I didn't want to go anywhere.

Or do anything.

A couple of times Mom suggested getting another rat. I shut her down fast.

Jenni tried to get me to go out with her and the stud muffin for pizza, invited me along when the Brittanys went to the movies, and even once offered to run with me.

Dad suggested we make our pilgrimage to the bookstore.

I said no to everything.

When I showed up at the store, Joan left me alone. She'd always have mindless and absorbing work for me to do: counting, unpacking, checking, restocking, vacuuming. She left gifts for me: one of those water-carrying belts with four small bottles, a pouch to hold my keys, a container of Kool-Aid-like drink. She said they were overstock and maybe I could use them. While my parents would have bought me anything I needed, the things Joan gave to me I treasured.

I thought about the story she'd told me on our run and wished I could be more like her, but I didn't have her strength, her endurance. I didn't think I could keep going.

9

Two weeks after Walter died I filled the bottles with water, poured in some of the powdered electrolyte mix, and strapped the belt on. I hoped not to run into Miles and Potato—I didn't want to have to explain what had happened—and I didn't.

I had become a creature of habit during the short time I'd been running. I liked always going the same way, always knowing how far I'd traveled and how much farther I had to get back. There were certain landmarks I looked forward to passing. I knew I'd usually be cold or creaky until I got to the capitol, but after that, I'd be warmed up and feeling loose. For some reason, I always held my breath when I ran by the power plant.

I hadn't done much exploring. My neophobia was acting up.

Since nothing felt good anyway, since there was no Bengay balm for the ache in my heart, no ointment to take away the sting, I decided that instead of turning around at my usual point, I would keep going.

The boulevard follows the Kanawha River. As I got farther from downtown, the path had more cracks in it;

tufts of grass and spring flowers pushed their way through the asphalt. Then it got narrow until it was no longer paved and was just a dirt trail. I kept running. The earth felt good under my shoes. I couldn't go as fast—less traction, more friction, some physics principle at work—but I didn't care.

Even though the ground was uneven, instead of looking down as I normally did, paying attention to where my feet were landing, I held my head high. I thought about Walter, about how he was always looking up. His approach to the world was, "Hey, what's that?" never, "Oh crap, now what?" He got excited whenever I brought anything new home. Especially paper bags. I think he loved the sound he made when he ran around in a paper bag. He also liked to climb on my running shoes whenever I got back from a run. Sometimes he'd just settle into one of them and sleep there.

I could see the 35th Street bridge in the distance. The trees were bursting with light green buds and white flowers. I could smell the dirt, heavy and rich.

I ran easily. I noticed how many birds were flitting around in the trees and I heard the sounds of the river. I felt fluid, strong. I picked up the pace, pumped my arms harder, made my lungs and legs and heart strain.

I got to the bridge and ran up the curly stairway that twisted to the pedestrian walkway. I ran across the bridge, feeling the heave of the cars as they zoomed by.

I hadn't brought a watch and had no idea how long I'd been out. I thought I should drink, but I wasn't thirsty.

I kept going.

There was no one around. It wasn't like running on the boulevard. On this side of the river I felt completely and totally alone.

Dogs barked in the distance, which made me think about Walter. Silent Walter. Walter, who never complained, never worried, was always in a good mood, even when he was old and sick. Walter, who hid his discomfort until he couldn't anymore. The vet had said rats have incredible capacity to handle pain. Walter, so sweet and gentle and so tough, so very tough. Once, early on, not long after I'd gotten him, he had fallen from my shoulder. I was terrified he had broken something. He shook himself off and commenced grooming.

I couldn't stop thinking about him, and a slideshow of pictures flashed through my head. I saw him when I first got him, the only time he was ever timid. I'd put an empty tissue box in his cage and he hid in it. He'd pop his head up, like the Whac-A-Mole game at the fair. I'd pet him on the white diamond on the top of his head and he'd duck back down. Seconds later, he'd pop up again. It turned into a game called Toaster. I'd hold my hand over the opening on the box and he'd stay down until I took it away. Then I'd remove my hand and say, "Ding!" And he'd spring up like a perfectly toasted bagel.

We also played Tarzan, where he'd grab on to a pencil I'd hold out parallel to the ground and would swing from it. "What a great ape," I'd say to him. "You are the very small King of the Jungle."

On my hands I had tiny scars where he had

accidentally scratched me. I loved those scars. I hoped they'd last forever. Thinking about that, worrying that the scars would fade, that I would stop being able to remember him, made me start to cry.

Running and crying was more difficult than just running. I could see the downtown bridge ahead and was surprised at how much ground I'd covered.

Then I couldn't run another step. My legs wouldn't go. I could barely swing my arms.

I slowed to a walk, and then just had to stop. This must have been what Nikki meant by "hitting the wall." I could not take another step.

I sat on the bank of the river and took one of the bottles off the belt. I glugged down a slug of jock juice and coughed it all back out. I kept coughing.

For a long time I sat on that rock and cried.

I didn't know how I was going to make it home.

I didn't feel like I could take another step. I barely had the energy to raise the bottle to my mouth. I was breathing hard, just sitting and not moving.

I thought about Joan, and about Miles, and about that runner Pre, their hero, who said he could take more pain than anyone.

I drank another bottle, more slowly so I didn't cough.

I got up and forced myself to run.

10

I usually just picked my way through dinner and then went right up to the guest room. Mom had tried to find ways to keep me around after we'd finished eating, like asking me questions.

You can imagine how well that worked.

But after dinner one night Dad called out, "What's a three-letter word for *goof*?"

"Err," I said, without really thinking.

He nodded. "Six letters for 'It has eyes that can't see'?"

I thought a minute. "Potato."

"Right-o."

"'Derisive look,' begins with *sn*?"

"Sneer."

Mom had settled on the couch with a copy of *Vogue*. The TV was on PBS, and a show started that I couldn't help but watch. It was called *What Are Animals Thinking?*

It profiled a bunch of scientists working on animal cognition. Researchers in Germany did a cool and simple experiment to find out whether dogs cared about fairness. A guy asked a dog for her paw. She gave it to him. He asked her about thirty times and each time, she gave it to him.

Then they brought in another dog and the guy asked that dog for his paw. The second dog gave the guy his paw and the guy said, "Good dog!" and gave him a treat. Then he asked the first dog, and when she gave him her paw, he didn't say anything or give her a treat.

They went back and forth like this for a while. The second dog got props and treats every time he gave his paw, and the first dog, sitting right next to him, doing the same work, had to watch and get nothing. After a short while, the first dog went on strike. If she could talk, she would have used the rallying cry of kids everywhere: "It isn't fair."

I hadn't meant to stay downstairs, but this show was really interesting.

There was also a segment about bonobos, which are like small chimps. The guy who talked about the experiment was a professor at Duke, and he seemed super-young and had crazy hair and I thought for a minute maybe I should have gone back on my anti-Duke stance and applied there, because I could totally imagine myself being his star student.

As soon as they heard the word *Duke*, both my parents looked up and started watching. Mom said something about the Lemur Center at Duke being the home of the largest collection of prosimian primates anywhere in the world. I knew this because I did a report on lemurs in middle school. I resisted the urge to say, *No shit.*

The absolute best part of the show was about rats. At the University of Chicago, researchers did a study that showed rats have empathy. On the one hand, my response to this was: *Duh*. Anyone who's ever spent time with a rat knows that. But they were looking at it scientifically.

They set up an experiment where two rats, cage-mates, were put into a bigger cage—they called it an arena. One of them was free to roam and the other was put into a clear plastic tube. The rat in the tube was not happy, and the other guy could tell. Once the free rat got comfortable in the arena, he learned how to open the door to let the "restrained" rat out. Then the scientists put a bunch of chocolate chips in the arena. The free rat had to decide whether to release the tubed rat or to chow down. Most of the time, he would release his friend. When he ate the chips, he left some for the other guy.

When the restrained rat got free, the rescuer would chase him around the cage, jumping on him and doing a victory dance.

The woman who did the experiment watched a video of the rats with the TV host and you could see on her face how proud the researcher was when the free guy opened the door for his imprisoned friend. She practically did a fist pump.

My mom said, "I never realized."

Dad reached over and rubbed my shoulder. "I miss him too," he said.

I continued to refuse to discuss my college plans with anyone. My teachers, especially Ms. Chan and Mr. Bergmann, asked what I was going to do, but I said I didn't know.

Sam Malouf, who won a scholarship to Northwestern, kept saying, "Where'd you get in, Rat Girl? Going to pahk your cah in Hah-vid yahd?" He was mad that I had beat him out for valedictorian.

I caught my mother and Jenni whispering together a bunch of times. I heard "her" and "she" and "decision" leak out from around corners and under closed doors and I knew they were talking about me.

Since that run to the far bridge, I had been running every day. But if I didn't go really fast, if I allowed my mind to wander, I would get upset.

So I ran until it hurt, and then kept going.

12

On a warm Sunday in mid-April, Walter-the-Man came into the house and hollered for me.

"Alice," he bellowed. I didn't respond.

After he called for me six more times I came downstairs. "What?"

"Let's go," he said.

"No."

"You don't even know where we're going."

"Don't care. Don't want to go anywhere."

"Not acceptable. Get a sweater and come on. And don't look at me in that tone of voice."

Mom was standing in the entryway watching us. He looked at her and said, "Basement?"

She nodded.

He disappeared down the stairs.

WTF?

I glanced at my mother. She shrugged and went into the kitchen.

When he came back Walter-the-Man was carrying one of my mother's golf clubs. I knew it was hers because it was wearing a hat Jenni had made for it.

"No way," I said.

"Way," Walter-the-Man said.

"I am not playing golf."

. "No, you're not. You don't know how to play golf. We're going to the driving range because I still have until midnight tomorrow to submit my taxes. Procrastination is a time-honored American tradition."

"No," I said, and crossed my arms.

Walter-the-Man opened the door. "Remember the old days when you were nice to me? Remember how you wanted to be the kind of person who would try anything once? Remember how you wanted to be more like Walter?"

I thought that was a low blow.

"Let's go," he said, and headed outside.

I sighed loudly, even though no one was there to hear it, and followed him.

"We're going in the MLC-mobile?" A few years ago Walter-the-Man had bought a red Porsche convertible, which I attributed to a midlife crisis and took every opportunity to point out.

"It's a chick magnet," he said, and pushed a button that made the top fold down.

Mom hated riding in the convertible because it messed up her hair. My hair was always messy anyway, so I didn't care. I could not believe he was kidnapping me like this. I said, "Stranger danger."

He put his fingers in his ears and said, "Lalalalalalalala."

We got to the country club, which I had always made

fun of for being elitist and tacky, and Walter-the-Man handed me my mom's golf club.

"We're going to smack some balls," he said.

And the only thing I could think of was Walter.

There's something about rats—about male rats—that's rather amazing. Well, another thing. It's that they have the biggest balls you've ever seen. Walter's nutsack was disproportionately large. Like, if he were a man he'd have testicles the size of cantaloupes. Or those award-winning pumpkins people grow for contests. I didn't think about them much, they were just a part of who he was, like his tiny four-fingered hands, his big pink feet, his dark round eyes.

But everyone who met Walter said something about his package. Having never seen a man's junk up close and in real life, I pretended it was no big deal.

When Walter-the-Man said, "balls," I thought of Walter, and I was afraid I was going to start crying. I didn't want him to see so I walked off toward the clubhouse and muttered something about needing to get a soda.

When I got back, Walter-the-Man had staked out a spot on the driving range and was swinging away but not hitting any balls.

He turned and saw me and said, "Step right up here, missy."

"Don't call me missy, bucko."

"Alice, get your club. Please."

I plucked Jenni's knitted hat, yellow with a black smiley face, off the club and held it like a baseball bat.

"Okay. Take your left arm, let it hang down naturally,

239

and then take hold of the club by the grip. Let your right arm hang loose and put your hand on the club. Good, good. Put the little finger of your right hand between the index and middle fingers of your left."

"That baseball hat is probably older than I am," I said, raising my chin toward his head. The hat, naturally, said *Duke*.

"Don't worry about that. Now, the stance. You want an athletic posture with a slight bend at the knees, a slight forward tilt at the waist, and your weight primarily on the balls of your feet.

"Put your left foot in line with the ball." He stuck a fluorescent orange tee into the ground in front of me and topped it with a new white ball. "The backswing," he said, and stepped away and did a slow and exaggerated motion with the club.

"When you pull the club back, it should stay facing the target for a good couple of feet or so."

"By 'target,' I assume you mean the ball?"

"Yes, the ball."

"Then why didn't you say ball?"

"The downswing begins with the lower body, not the hands or arms. This is one of the hardest things to groove—"

I snorted when he said, "groove," and he ignored me.

"—since it feels natural at this point to take a hack at the ball. That will not end well. You rotate, starting with your hips, and then sort of let your shoulders, then your arms, and then finally your hands, catch up."

"How long will this lecture last?"

"Finally, the follow-through and finish position. Your back foot should come up only after you've struck the ball and should end up resting on the toe of your shoe, and your belt buckle needs to be facing the target."

I told him:

1. "I don't wear a belt. Ever.
2. "If I did, it wouldn't have some big old buckle.
3. "Haven't we already established the target is a ball?"

I said, "Why can't you just call it a ball, like the way they do in, say, baseball or even basketball or even football where the ball is not even ball-shaped?"

"Alice," Walter-the-Man said, "just take a goddamn swing."

I did. I didn't think of any of the things he'd said, and swatted. I didn't hit the ball; I whacked a big chunk out of the nicely manicured lawn and ended up spinning myself around and nearly walloping Walter-the-Man with my club.

"Oops."

"Try again," he said.

The second time, I dug up another big clump of dirt, but the third time, I smacked the ball with a satisfying *thwack*, and the sucker soared. It flew up and, like a bird of prey, dove back down.

Walter-the-Man said nothing and put another ball on the tee.

I swung again and hit it again. Not as far, but I hit it.

The next time I took a swing, I whacked the tee right out from under the ball. The tee went sailing and the ball just plopped down two inches so that it was sitting on the ground and not the tee.

"I've never seen anyone do that," Walter-the-Man said.

I picked up the broken tee. "You've never played golf with me before."

"We're not playing golf," he said.

There were so many things to think about, big things, like how to maintain your body position, and small things, like keeping your eye on the tee and not looking up to see where the ball goes—assuming it actually goes somewhere—that I didn't think of anything else for three whole hours. Every time I connected with the ball felt like a triumph.

Hearing that *thwack* never got old.

Of course, I didn't hear it every time. Or even every other time. And I still managed to spin myself around occasionally. I wanted more tips. I wanted to know what I was doing wrong. Walter-the-Man would feed me little things: "Breathe before you swing. Inhale. Then exhale. Then swing." Mostly he just said, "Nice," and teed up another ball. When we were finished, the green was more brown than green because I had dug up so much dirt.

"I thought golf was just a bunch of paunchy guys riding around in go-carts," I said as we walked back to the MLC-mobile. "I'm tired. My arms are sore and so are my legs."

I knew my parents went to the country club occasionally—less now than they did when I was young—but I never knew what it would be like to play. Walter-the-Man said, "Your mother is an excellent golfer. Your dad's okay, but he's not in your mom's league. Literally. She's won the women's title before. She doesn't like to play because you can't win at this game."

"You just said she won."

"You can never beat the game. It will always beat you. It's the most frustrating thing in the world. Your mother likes to do things where she's a clear winner."

He pulled his hat low on his forehead and added, "You might know something about what that's like."

13

After my parents and I watched the TV show about rats, I got a little obsessed and started doing even more rat research. I was supposed to write a final paper for psychology class but realized that I wasn't all that interested in people.

So I started Googling around for things written by psychologists about rats. I found an article in a scientific journal about this experiment where a researcher learned that if you tickle rats, they laugh. Well, they emit *ultrasonic* ("at a frequency above human hearing") chirps.

The experiment seemed obvious to me, though it turned out to be kind of controversial. I found articles about it all over the place—including in *People* and *News of the Weird*. Why was this such a big deal? I mean, I couldn't hear Walter giggle when I tickled him—you needed the special electronic equipment to be able to hear the chirps— but I *knew* he was laughing. You could see it in his whole body.

From biology class, I learned that about the worst thing you can do in science is commit the "sin" of anthropomorphism. That's how they talk about it too—as a sin. Like adultery or baby-shaking or swindling old ladies out of their life savings. There are tons of scientists who just plain don't believe animals have emotions.

I might not be able to prove it scientifically, but with animals, it's usually easier to know what they're feeling than it is with people.

When I did some reading on this I found a book by Charles Darwin called *The Expression of the Emotions in Man and Animals* where he told a whole bunch of stories that show animals have emotions. He said there are universal emotions, expressed across species and cultures, and you could read them in people's and animals' faces.

Most nights I can get my homework done quickly. And I always get A's. But I spent a lot of time on that research paper and it turned out to be three times as long as it was supposed to be.

My psychology teacher, Mr. Krystal, gave me an A+++ on it and said he thought I'd found my calling.

Even after the paper was finished, I kept researching.

I flashed back to the time I showed Jenni photos of rats and she got all excited by the Dumbos.

"They're so cute," she said in a high squeaky voice.

"Cuter than Walt?"

"I mean, look at that round face and those big round ears."

"Why is that cuter than Walter?"

"Because, oh, I don't know, it's just cute."

I started thinking about what makes something cute. I stumbled on this essay by a famous Harvard scientist named Stephen Jay Gould about how originally Mickey Mouse the cartoon character looked more like a rat.

Over the years Mickey's head got bigger and more childlike, his nose got thicker and less pointy, and his eyes went from being simple black dots to having pupils. His ears moved back on his head, farther from his nose, giving him a rounded rather than a sloped forehead. His former ratlike appearance changed into the bland profile of a little kid.

Gould quoted some German scientist about how animals with baby features—big heads, big eyes, bulging cheeks, pudgy arms and legs, and clumsy movements—triggered adults to want to care for them. In other words, we see those blobby things and it makes us go *"awww"* and speak in a high voice. Like the noises Jenni made when she saw the Dumbo rats.

Gould's point about how we are drawn to animals who look like babies explains not only why some people don't appreciate rats, but also why hamsters, those tiny terrorists, are so popular. They're fat and round and cute. They also eat their own babies and bite the people who feed them.

14

I uncovered all sorts of rat facts:

1. Queen Victoria loved rats. Jack Black, a famous rat catcher, gave rats to the fancy people of the time. That's why pet rats are called fancy rats.
2. During the Roman Empire, it was considered good luck for a white rat to cross your path. A black rat, not so much.
3. In rat terminology, *bucks* and *does* mate to produce *kittens*.
4. It is illegal to have pet rats in Billings, Montana. It is also illegal to have a sheep in the cab of your truck without a chaperone, and for married women to go fishing alone on Sundays.
5. One pair of rats can produce 15,000 descendants in a year. Male rats can do it for six hours at a time and most female rats in the wild are continuously pregnant.

6. Rats can squeeze into any hole they can get their head through.

7. Rats don't pant. They release heat through the bottoms of their (big) feet.

8. According to the U.S. Department of Agriculture, rats (along with mice and birds) are not considered "animals." There's an exception to the Animal Welfare Act, which provides guidelines of care for researchers and farmers, that excludes rats. Un-freaking-believable, but true. Rats, mice, and birds don't have to be treated in the same humane way as other animals.

9. It took until nearly the twentieth century before anyone knew what caused the Black Death. Alexandre Yersin found the bacteria responsible for the bubonic plague, and the name of the disease was changed from a description of what happened (you grew buboes, or lumps) to *Yersinia pestis*, in honor of the guy who figured out that the bug appeared in people who were bitten by rats, who, as we know, were bitten by fleas, who were the delivery system. So it's only been about a century we've been blaming rats for plague, and that's not even right, since the real culprits were the fleas.

Who got blamed for plague before anyone knew it was

carried by fleas on rats? Jews. Who else? Foreigners, beggars, and lepers. The usual suspects—the people at the margins. Prejudice and bigotry depend on ignorance to survive.

Maybe that's why I was so attracted to rats—aside from the part about loving Walter. I felt a connection to those who are marginal.

The popular kids made me nervous. They wore their "normal" like outfits. I could never find anything that would make me fit in with them.

So I colonized Jenni. I made her my territory. Often, when she was with the Brittanys, I engaged in competitive friendship. In any random conversation, I might insert something that proved I knew Jenni better than anyone else. If we were going to get ice cream, I'd point out that Jenni's favorite flavor was mint chocolate chip. I'd talk about the jewelry box she made for my mother. Sometimes, when I was feeling really threatened, like when Tiffany was making plans for a double date with her Neanderthal boyfriend and Jenni and Kyle, I'd mention Jenni's mom.

I'd also bring up things Jenni had told me about them. I'd say to Tiffany, "So how's your brother's knee healing?" even though I'd never met the brother. I'd ask Brittney if she'd finally finished reading *Fifty Shades of Grey*. The message was clear: Jenni is *my* best friend. She tells me everything. Don't even try to compete with me on this because I will crush you.

But it also made me appear to be interested in what the Brittanys were up to and I thought this made it okay. Sometimes they would look at me like, *How do you know this stuff and why are you bringing it up?*

Sometimes I probably came off as a bit of a stalker.

There were, though, parts of Jenni I didn't understand or even know much about. She was big into Facebook and Twitter and Instagram and had about a zillion friends and followers. She was always mentioning something she'd seen on some site, or using my computer to show me an unbearably cute video of an animal. I pretended I didn't care about any of this. I pretended I didn't want to go to football or basketball or baseball games with Jenni and the Brittanys and paint my face and scream my head off for Kyle and the Charleston High School Wasps. I said it was an insipid waste of time. (*Insipid* was an SAT word I got fond of and tend to overuse.)

I said I'd rather spend my nights at home reading a novel than going to a party on state land where someone had brought a keg and everyone stands around outside drinking and disappearing into the woods to make out.

I'd made such a big deal of my opinions on this stuff I felt like I couldn't back down from them.

Part of me kind of *did* want to go to games and drink beer—even though I hate football and can't stand the taste of beer—and smooch with a boy and talk about what everyone was wearing to prom and who hooked up with people who weren't their dates.

But I proclaimed my marginality so much and so loudly I got stuck with it.

15

Out on the www I found all these sites for professors at different universities who were doing research with rats on animal behavior and emotion. Some were in psychology departments, some in biology, some in neuroscience, and some in health sciences and even veterinary schools.

The site I loved the most belonged to a professor at a small college in Boston I'd never heard of. There were all these photos of her with rats that had markings similar to Walter's. You could tell she liked working with them. She'd written a book called *Tales of the Laboratory Rat* and I ordered it for my e-reader and started devouring it. She said that we could learn a lot from rats. Not just the usual stuff—like for science and medicine—but about how to live, things like emotional resilience and having a strong work ethic and developing effective parenting skills and staying healthy. She maintained that the lab rat is an unlikely but powerful role model. She told stories of experiments her students had helped to design.

In fact, on her Web site she had a whole page of the biographies of students who had worked with her as undergrads and gone on to graduate school in neuroscience, biological psychology, neurobiology, clinical psychology, pediatrics, criminal justice, and veterinary medicine.

Not only that, she was a runner. She had links to her favorite races, including a bunch of marathons and a whole bunch of ultramarathons—the races longer than 26.2 miles.

On a Wednesday after school, when I should have been studying differential equations and trying to understand the meaning of the Arch of Constantine, I decided that I would be more focused if I went for a run.

I started missing Walter like crazy. He was always so happy when I came back and kicked off my running shoes so he could play in them. He really liked it when they were sweaty and stinky and that had made me want to run more. It was easier when I believed I was doing something for him.

Thinking about Walter made me start out too fast.

I was trying to run away from my sadness and it caught up. After only about a mile, I was already winded and hurting.

So I slowed down.

I imagined that the sadness could leave my body through my sweat, that with every exhale I was breathing out the grief and loss I'd been holding on to.

I thought about that scientist's Web site. How cool would it be to work with rats?

During the last part of the run, I thought about writing a letter to her. Before I knew it, I was back at home, sitting at the computer, looking at her Web site again. I clicked on the Contact button, and there was her e-mail address. I clicked on the address and had a blank e-mail ready to go, just like that. So I wrote to her.

To: Marnie Horowitz
Subject: Rodentiaphilia

Dear Professor Horowitz,

This may seem like a crazy, out-of-the-blue message, but I found your Web site, have read most of your book, and wanted to thank you for making me happy during a really difficult time.

This year I was rejected Early Action by my first-choice college (Yale), and then rejected from almost every other college I applied to (not enough extracurricular activities, nothing special about me, though I had excellent grades and test scores, yada yada yada), and then my rat, Walter, died. I know I don't have to explain to you how great rats are. I'm a rodentiaphile, which is a word I made up to express how much I love rats. (As I'm sure you know, rats are in the order Rodentia; *phile* means "one that loves.")

Walter was fearless and friendly, he tried new things but was cautious enough never to get hurt. He was always in a good mood. I am not always in a good mood and, recently, I've been wallowing in my own misery. I've tried to be more like Walter but in that, as with everything lately, I've been failing.

Just wanted to let you know that finding your Web page was one of the few highlights I've had recently. I've been doing a ton of research on animal behavior and emotion, and have been reading the textbook *Affective Neuroscience* by Jaak Panksepp. I guess his big thing is describing the brain circuits in rats that are similar to those of humans. If we have similar neurochemical pathways, why wouldn't we have similar emotions? I'm surprised people think his findings about rats giggling when they are tickled are controversial—anyone who's ever spent five minutes with rats knows they have deep emotional lives. And that's what Darwin thought, right?

Sorry. I'm rambling. I get all fired up about this stuff and then go on and on and bore everyone around me.

Sincerely,
Alice Davis

P.S.: Also, I saw that you are a runner. I started running this year.

16

Jenni brought her prom dress over. It had turned out incredible.

She'd eighty-sixed the bow in the front and had replaced it with a band of fabric, textured and intricate and delicately pretty. When she tried it on, she glowed like a *Project Runway* model who had already been to the L'Oréal Paris Makeup Room.

We went downstairs to the kitchen to show my mother, who looked at it, yelped, and said, "Wait right here." I knew she was running up to the shoe sanctuary. She came down with a pair of strappy high-heeled sandals hanging from her finger.

"These will be perfect." She presented them to Jenni with a kiss on the head. "Wear them well."

Jenni squealed.

Then she looked at the brand—a brand that even I recognized as crazy expensive—and tried to hand them back to my mother. She said, "Sarah, I can't."

Mom said, "Jenni, honey. I got them, tried them on, and they just don't fit. But they were on sale. On supersale. I didn't send them back because I thought that one day they might come in handy."

"Or footy," I said, but no one was paying any attention to me.

"If you don't want them, they're going to Goodwill," Mom said. "But it would be a shame because, I mean, they're perfect for this dress."

And they were.

Not much more than a couple strips of leather—very expensive, very soft leather—they matched exactly the blue and black of Jenni's dress.

I remembered that not long after Jenni first showed Mom the sketch and a swatch of the dress material, I saw a shoe box from Zappos in the front hallway.

Jenni said, "Thank you so much."

Mom grabbed her and threw an arm around me as well. "Group hug," she said.

Normally I'd squirm out of this kind of huddle, but Jenni was so happy about the shoes and the dress and going to prom I allowed myself to be swallowed up in their corny embrace. For a few seconds.

"I wish you'd come," Jenni said to me when I'd had enough and shook myself like a wet dog.

"I. Am. Never. Going. To. Prom," I said. "Could I be more clear?"

"You could ask Miles," Jenni said, and Mom looked at me and I could tell if she could have, she would have hoisted her eyebrows to her hairline.

"Right."

When it was obvious I would entertain no more discussion about this, Mom said, "Dad's out of town that weekend. You and I can get some M&M's and a movie."

"Peanut," I said.

"What?" Mom said.

"They have to be peanut M&M's," I said.

"What else would they be? Everything else is a pretender."

I tried to be really casual when I said, "Can we watch a movie called *Harold and Maude*?"

I generally vetoed all of her suggestions and rarely had any of my own. We'd spend so much time trying to figure out what to watch that often it got so late we ended up settling on an episode of *The Real Housewives of Beverly Hills*. Which was kind of fun, because Mom liked to point out the many ways their procedures had gone bad—too much Restylane in the lips, Botox in the wrong places.

Mom cocked her head and said, "Sure."

But she seemed unsure.

She said, "I haven't seen it in years. I used to love that movie." I could see her thinking. "I wonder if it's the best—I mean, right now might not be—"

She stopped.

She glanced at Jenni, who was no help because:

1. I knew she hadn't seen *Harold and Maude*.
2. She was busy caressing the straps of her new shoes.

3. If I didn't know what the problem was, why
   did my mom think Jenni would?

Then Mom said, "Yes, let's watch it. That sounds great."
Jenni, in her prom dress, in those altitude-sickness
high heels, beamed. Nothing seemed to make her happier
than when my mom and I got along.

Then Mom looked at Jenni and said, "Wait."

She left again, and while she was upstairs, Jenni and I
tried dancing in the kitchen. She was able to walk and
yes, even to dance, in those strappy shoes.

This time Mom came in holding a small quilted leather
purse with two interlocking *C*'s, one backward and one
normal, on it.

"This is a loaner, not a gift."

Jenni yipped and did a cheerleading leap, and I was
afraid we were going to have a serious shoe injury.

"Wear them well," I said to Jenni.

My mother smiled.

So I said, "And if you break your leg, I'll decorate your
cast."

Jenni said, "Alice, you can be a real downer, but I love
you anyway."

And then the three of us rocked out to imaginary music.

17

On prom night, Mom and I helped Jenni get ready. Well, Mom helped and I cracked jokes.

Her dad had stopped drinking again—at least temporarily—and he'd gotten Jenni a flower thingy, which Mom pinned to her dress.

By the time Kyle picked Jenni up at our house, she looked better than Heidi Klum.

Since Dad was out of town, Mom made us eggs with hats for dinner. It was one of the few things she could cook.

Eggs with hats are not something you find on restaurant menus. It's kid food. Even though I'd seen my mom make it a thousand times, I would never cook it for myself. Eggs with hats is the kind of food that only tastes right when someone else makes it for you. Someone like your mom.

First you take a slice of bread—I prefer white bread, the unhealthy kind, but you can use any type. Sometimes, when she wants to get fancy, Mom will substitute sourdough, and when she's on a health kick, the multigrain kind with lots of seeds.

You take a glass and use it as a cookie cutter to punch

out a hole in the middle of the slice of bread. Then you put butter in a pan and you fry the bread—plus the circle made by the hole—and crack an egg into the cutout space. It's tricky, because you have to cook the egg to the perfect consistency and then flip it and not break the yoke.

Then you put it on a plate, the bread with the egg in the hole and the cutout bread, which you put on top of where it used to be. That's the hat. If it's cooked right, the egg will be slightly runny, and you can use the hat to soak up extra yolk.

Once when we were having it Jenni said, "Why is this called eggs with hats? Isn't it that the whole thing, when you put the circle on top, becomes a hat? It's hat eggs."

"Stop talking now," I said.

You don't mess with someone's childhood by trying to come up with reasons for why things are called what they're called. "This is an egg with a hat. Period."

I later learned that some people call them other things, like toad in the hole, or egg in a hole, or piggies in a basket, or even picture-frame eggs or window eggs. That's all just wrong.

They're called eggs with hats and that's that, people.

Jenni said they were delicious. But sometimes, when she was feeling frisky and wanted to tweak me, she'd whisper, "The egg is the hat."

Mom and I took our plates of eggs with hats into the living room. We also had glasses of fresh-squeezed orange juice, going with the whole breakfast-for-dinner motif, and Mom made some bacon, cooked so it was crispy and not at all rubbery. Dad likes it slimy but Mom and I both like it cooked to within an inch of its life.

We put the pound bag of peanut M&M's into a crystal bowl for the sake of elegance and queued up the movie.

Before she hit Play, Mom touched my arm and said, "Why did you pick this one?"

I didn't want to tell her about Miles, so I raised my palms and said I'd heard it was good.

After it started, I was uncertain.

The kid, Harold, tried to kill himself twice in the first seven minutes, and then tried about fifty-seven more times.

Mom kept looking at me during the movie. I knew she was worried that a movie about death, about a young guy obsessed with death, might not be the right thing for me. I didn't look at her—just kept my eyes focused on the screen.

The music was amazing, all these great Cat Stevens songs. When Harold went to a funeral and saw Maude, who was a week away from her eightieth birthday, a woman so delightful and full of life, and Cat Stevens sang, "Miles from Nowhere," I gasped.

I think Mom thought I was upset because they were at a funeral.

But no.

I loved the idea that Miles, my Miles, who lived with his hippie parents out of town and off the grid, was Miles from Nowhere.

Maude was maybe the most beautiful old woman I'd ever seen. The wrinkles on her face, the light in her eyes, the way she twitched her mouth when she was being all flirty—you could only watch her the way Harold did, with awe and admiration and love.

By the end, I had to cover my face with a napkin because I was crying. I snuck a look at Mom and saw her cheeks were wet with tears. She had her hand on her forehead and her shoulders shook.

As Cat Stevens sang out at the end, Mom reached for me, and this time I let her hold me. I kept thinking of when Harold said, "I love you."

And Maude, beautiful Maude, wise and amazing Maude, told him that was wonderful, and that he should go and love some more.

Exactly what Walter would have said.

Walter and Maude were a lot alike.

18

Now that the weather was good all the time, it was easy to go for runs.

I found myself waiting until late in the afternoon because I liked looking forward to it and if I ran too early, I'd be disappointed it was already over and I wouldn't know what to do with myself after. School had gotten ridiculously easy once AP exams were over.

And running was going well, most of the time.

I still had bad days, days when it felt like I was harnessed to a thousand-pound weight that I had to drag behind me, and days when I didn't feel warmed up until just before I was finished. But a lot of the time I was able to cruise happily along.

I felt like a real runner. I'd been going farther and farther. If I planned to be out for a long time, I carried water with me. I learned from Joan to monitor the color of my pee. Dark pee means you're dehydrated. I had an impressive collection of socks with the Runner's Edge logo, but I tended to wear the same pair—and the same pair of shorts—and wash them out in the shower. When my nose started to drip, I held one nostril and blew out the snot the way

Miles had done. Or I wiped it on my sleeve and didn't care. I never hit the wall again, though after a couple of my longest runs, all I could do in the afternoon was lie in the hammock on the back deck and sigh. I stayed outside because I still didn't like being in my room.

I hadn't seen Miles since we ran together the day Walter died, though each time I came into the store, Joan would say, "Oh you just missed Miles." I had started thinking about him again, and for a nanosecond I wondered if he would have said yes if I had asked him to the prom.

A nanosecond later I realized he was the kind of kid who might hate prom as much or even more than I did.

A nanosecond after that I thought, I hardly know him. I don't know what he'd like or not like.

Just as I was finishing my Saturday-morning shift and had gone to the stockroom to change into my running clothes so I could jog home, I heard the door jingle.

A bunch of runners, mostly men and a few women, came in like a pack of stray dogs, skinny and hungry-looking in tiny shorts and flashing lean arms and messy hair. I saw the mass of red curls that belonged to Nikki and heard her unmistakable laugh.

"Need water," Nikki said. "Who knew it was going to be so hot this morning?"

"Weather.com?" said Joan, as she went over to the water cooler and started filling paper cups for the sweaty runners.

Nikki said, "Thanks, Joanie. You're always here when we need you," and she gulped the water so fast that it ended up dribbling down her chin. She wiped her face with the back of her hand and then said, "Okay, crew, let's go. Saturday morning run's not over until"—she glanced at a short woman with her hair in two pigtails—"we get the baked goods!" and with waves and grunts goodbye, they filed out the door.

Everyone except Miles.

"Alice," he said. "Hey."

"Hey," I said.

I wore a short-sleeved shirt and a pair of running shorts Joan had tossed at me saying, "Sale!" They had built-in underpants and I wasn't sure if I was supposed to wear anything beneath them. I had asked Joan and she said it was totally up to me. Some people did, some didn't. I did. My legs were still Clorox-commercial white, but when I looked down at them I noticed how after only four months, they'd become more muscular.

I'd seen my body develop and get stronger. Nothing much jiggled on me anymore. My thighs were still big, but they were solid. My gluteus maximus had gotten only a little less maximus, but like my thighs, my butt was hard and no longer Jell-O-like.

Right after Walter's death I hadn't been eating much, and I'd felt myself getting weak. But since I'd started running longer distances, I'd built back up. I felt strong.

Miles said, "You look really good."

Gulp.

"I'm headed toward the boulevard for my warm down. Wanna?"

"Sure," I said.

19

"Miles from nowhere," I said when we'd started to run.

"You saw it!" Miles said.

I nodded, even though we were running side by side and he couldn't see me.

"What parts did you like best?"

"You mean besides everything?"

He laughed. "Including everything."

I told him there wasn't anything I didn't like about it, but my favorite part was when Harold and Maude were sitting together and Harold says to Maude that she has a way with people and Maude just kind of shrugs and says, "Well, they're my species," and he gives her a present and it says . . .

Miles chimed in and we said the line together. I thought how right Maude was that if you toss the material stuff away, you'll always know where it is and you can hold on to the feeling instead.

We were running pretty fast, but it felt good. At times we were even running in step, like a pair of horses harnessed together.

He said, "God, I love that movie. Can you believe it's

more than forty years old? The woman who played Maude, Ruth Gordon, was also a screenwriter. She and her husband, Garson Kanin, wrote one of Harry's favorite movies—*Adam's Rib*, with Katharine Hepburn and Spencer Tracy. It's about a married couple, both lawyers, who end up on opposing sides of a case. Wouldn't be a big deal, except that it was made in 1949 when there weren't many women lawyers and Katharine Hepburn's character makes an argument about treating women equally."

He was geeking out. It was really cute.

"That's your kind of movie?"

"You bet. Harry is a feminist from way back. It rubs off."

"But you're also kind of a romantic?"

"Not mutually exclusive," he said.

"Too bad you have such bad taste in books."

He turned to look at me, but I kept my eyes straight ahead. "No one's ever said that to me before."

"*The Catcher in the Rye*? Really?"

"What's your problem with *Catcher*?"

He asked it as a real question, not a challenge.

So I told him.

I told him all the stuff I'd written in my crappy college-admission essay about how Holden was a big phony, how he was all polite to people to their faces but he went around judging everyone, and it wasn't fun to be in the head of someone who was pissed off at the world all the time. Teenage rage wasn't that interesting. He was a hypocrite and I can't stand hypocrisy.

Miles slowed and said, "Hmmm. I read it a little differently from you. I don't think it's just about teenage rage. I think it's about something else."

"Yeah? What's that?"

"Death," he said. "Dealing with death."

That stopped me. Literally. I stopped running. So Miles did too.

"Think about it," Miles said. "Where is Holden at the beginning of the book?"

I tried to remember. I started running again and Miles fell in beside me. "At that fancy prep school he'd just been kicked out of."

"No," said Miles.

"Yes he was. And he went to see his English teacher, who had the grippe." I have to confess that after reading that book, whenever I got a cold, I said I had the grippe.

"No," said Miles again, patiently, like a teacher. "He was writing down all the crazy stuff that happened. It was because he was in the same place he was at the end of the book. In the loony bin. Right? He'd been having all this trouble at school, and made that wild trip to New York because—"

"Because he was still so upset about his brother's death," I said, "which was, like, years before."

"Three years before, when he first started having trouble in school."

I hadn't thought about that.

I'd read the book before I lost Walter—before anyone I'd

ever loved had died—and I hadn't understood how grief makes you more angry than sad, how you can't control your behavior, can't control your thoughts.

I had missed the main message of *The Catcher in the Rye.*

It was a book about grief.

20

My last day at the store wasn't as sad as I thought it would be because Joan told me I had to come in on Saturday mornings for the group run. I knew Nikki and Miles and other speedy people always showed up, but Joan promised there would be people who ran my pace. She said, "Caroline runs about an eleven-minute mile, and you're a lot quicker than that."

"Miles is pretty great," I said. And then felt embarrassed and busied myself dusting the counter.

"He is," she said. "You are too. Guess it runs in the family. Your mom—you know this. Your mom is an incredible doctor. And a wonderful person. I don't know what we would have done without her."

I finally felt like I knew Joan well enough to ask her. "So did my mom find a mole? On Ricardo?"

Joan exhaled. "No, not a mole."

"Sorry. I was just wondering."

"No, it's okay. Your mother is really the hero, so you should hear it."

"My mother? A hero? I mean, I know the women whose

wrinkles my mom erases worship her, but it's all cosmetic. Not important stuff."

Joan sat down on the bench that faced the START wall and patted the spot next to her. I settled in beside her. We both looked at the wall blanketed with bib numbers for a while, and then, finally, she began to speak in a soft voice.

"I've known your mother for a long time. Someone with skin like mine"—she extended her pale arm in front of her, dotted with freckles and moles—"who spends as much time outdoors as I do, I knew it was important to keep an eye on things.

"Ricardo, on the other hand, was dark, and didn't like going to doctors. He began to suffer from back pain. He'd had a bike crash, not terrible, not for a cyclist at least, and assumed that's what it was from. After about a year, I got him to go to a doctor, and the doc said it was nothing. Said he should do exercises to strengthen the muscles that support his back, that many people have weak backs. Ricardo tried to explain he didn't think that was the problem, but the doctor wouldn't listen."

Joan choked out a laugh. "Ricardo's back was stronger than anyone's. He wasn't a whiner, never complained about pain." She rubbed her hands over her slim hips.

"Then he got these purple dots on his lower eyelid. One day, when I was seeing your mom for my mole check, I told her what was going on with him. At the end of the day, she stopped by the store and said she wanted to take a look at Ricardo's face. She talked to him for a while, asked a bunch of questions, and said to us, 'I'm afraid I know what this is.' She explained she had trained in oncology and people tend to diagnose from within their specialty but—"

"She didn't train in oncology. She's a dermatologist."

Joan kept going. "She said she had been through an oncology residency and she'd seen this before. She said the spots were purpuras and that, with the joint pain, she was worried Ricardo might have multiple myeloma, a cancer of the blood. She sent him to a friend of hers who is an oncologist—"

"Sylvia," I said, interrupting, and then felt bad about interrupting.

"Sylvia," Joan said, nodding.

"And sure enough, your mom was right. Ricardo had to go through radiation therapy and chemo and even a stem cell transplant. He was so strong," Joan said, and her voice wavered. "It was awful. For him, the worst part was not having that first doctor take him seriously. Ricardo knew his body. He knew what muscle pain was and he knew this was different. Your mom didn't doubt him for a minute."

She fiddled with her necklace. "He died four and a half years later."

"Oh god," I said.

"Before he died, I got to tell him everything I wanted him to know. How much I loved him." She swallowed. "How he'd helped me to refocus my life, to learn to enjoy things and give up being tortured by my own competitiveness.

Even though the treatments were rough, we had Sylvia and your mom with us all along the way. He liked Sylvia, but boy was he crazy about Sarah."

I wondered where I was during all of this. Ricardo must have been diagnosed around the time Jenni's mom had died. Of cancer. And my mother's own mom had died of cancer.

Joan said, "You may think what she does is cater to wealthy women who care about their appearance, but your mother is one of the finest people I've ever known— smart, capable, and caring. You'd be hard-pressed to find a better role model, Alice."

21

That night, when Mom was reading *Vanity Fair* magazine, I asked, "How do you know Joan?"

She looked at me kind of funny. Then she said, "I can't
tell you that."

"She already told me she was a patient of yours. She also
told me about Ricardo. And about what you did for him."

She turned a page of *Vanity Fair* without reading it.

"I didn't do anything for him," she said quietly. "I wish
I could have."

"Joan told me," I said, insistent. "She said you figured out what was wrong with him after his own doctor
couldn't."

She looked in my eyes as if there was something lost in
them.

"She told me you were trained in oncology. That's not
true. Is it?"

She put down the magazine. She held her hand in front
of her and examined her French manicure. The white
half-moons on the tips of her fingernails caught the light.

"Yes," she said, after a long pause. "Originally I wanted
to be an oncologist. After my mother died, I was determined

to find a cure for cancer. Or many cures for the many different cancers. I was young."

She glanced up and to the side, as if to excuse her own silly thoughts. Then she continued. "I got into an onc residency at Duke. When I was nearly finished with my third year, Dr. Agrawal, my mentor—the woman I hoped to become—took me aside and said, 'This is not the right field for you.' I thought she was telling me I wasn't good enough. She said no, it wasn't that I couldn't do the work, but what the work was doing to me. I got too attached to the patients, many of whom were very, very sick. I'd sit with them for too long and run late, and when they died— and most of them died—I'd be destroyed. Residency's no picnic, but I was more ragged than most."

"Her photo. On your dresser?"

She nodded. "I was Dr. Agrawal's star student. She was a consummate clinician and was also doing important research. I thought I'd have a job with her when my residency was over. She said she wouldn't hire me. She said it would do me in."

I couldn't imagine my fierce mother not getting a job she wanted. I thought she'd always gotten everything she'd ever wanted. I didn't interrupt, just listened.

"Dr. Agrawal steered me toward dermatology. She said I'd have lots of happy patients and would be able to treat them over many years. She knew how much my mother's death had affected me. She also knew I was always going to choose the hardest path and she thought it was unhealthy. I dismissed the whole idea until she told me dermatology was the most competitive residency to get into."

She laughed. "Funny, right? I worry about how hard you push yourself and worry that you're never satisfied with anything less than perfect."

I wondered how I hadn't known this before.

I knew my parents had met at Bowdoin, their cozy college in Maine, and had both gone to graduate school at Duke, where I was born. The only stories I had wanted to hear from them were about me, about after I'd come onto the scene. I hadn't really thought of my parents—especially my mother—as people who had lives before me.

"As it turns out, I love derm," she said. "I love being able to fix things. Because I've seen so many cases, I can, often in the blink of an eye, recognize patterns and make diagnoses that general practitioners miss. I love that I get to check in with people for so many years, see them grow up and age, hear their stories, become a part of their lives. And, even though I know you don't approve, I like being able to make people feel better about the way they look. It makes them happy, and I'd rather see happy patients than people in pain who are going to die anyway."

I listened and said, "I never knew."

She said, "You never asked."

22

The next day, when Jenni and I were at the Coffee Shop after school, I said, "Get this. My mom started out as a cancer doc."

Jenni said, "Yeah."

"What?"

"I know. She's told me all about it. She worshipped Dr. Agrawal."

"*What?* Why'd she tell you, not me?"

Jenni stared into her double mocha caramel cappuccino and blew on it until some foam floated up and landed on the table.

Finally she said, "I don't know, Al. Maybe she thought you'd judge her."

I stopped eating the chocolate chip scone I'd been craving, the whole reason we'd gone to the Coffee Shop.

"She thinks you don't approve of her. She thinks you look down on her choices—not just about career, but about everything."

"Since when does Sarah Davis give a hoot about what anyone thinks of her?"

"I guess since she had a daughter who cares even less."

"When did she tell you all this?"

"Geez, I don't know. Over the past few years. You think we only talk about shoes and makeup, but when we drink coffee in the kitchen while you're playing with Walter"—she broke off, but I motioned with my hand that it was okay—"when we go on shopping trips, mostly what we do is talk. Sure, we look at clothes and we experiment with testers at the Chanel counter, but wandering around department stores gives you a lot of time for conversation."

"You talk about me?" It came out sounding like an accusation.

"Of course," she said, and laughed. "You're the most important person in each of our lives."

I didn't know whether to feel betrayed or flattered. Mostly, I was surprised.

"Alice," she said. "We love you. And we know you love us in your own sometimes obnoxious and self-absorbed way, though you're better at showing that to me than you are to your mother. You push her away. It's hard for her."

"You're *my* friend."

"We talk about lots of things. You don't really like to hear about Kyle and you tend to say mean things about Tiffany. And there's other stuff." She looked into her cup.

I thought about Jenni's face after her mother died. And about how she didn't like to be at home when her dad was drinking.

"I'm lucky to have her. It's like you and Walter-the-Man. I mean, he's okay, but I find him a little—"

"A little what?" I said, prepared to defend Walter-the-Man.

She hesitated.

"Intimidating. The two of you together are a force of nature. There's no room for anyone else when you guys are going at it."

She pointed to my scone and said, "Are you going to eat that?"

Even though I still wanted it, I pushed the plate over to her.

23

Joan was right: I was not the slowest person on the Saturday-morning group run.

Nikki and Miles and a tall balding computer programmer named Owen, who cracked jokes that were snarky but funny, and a few other guys whose names I didn't learn, were the speedy group, but there were a bunch of other people there as well.

After the first ten minutes the runners spread out and the fast ones got far ahead, though you could hear Nikki's laugh for a long time. I ended up running with Candace, a graphic designer, and Jeff, a professor of economics who used to be fast, he said, but was recovering from knee surgery, and Valerie, who ran a local nonprofit, and Ruth, who seemed to own a lot of property, and David, who was fast but thought the conversation at the back of the pack was more interesting. We ran slow and did a lot of talking.

It was amazing how much easier it was to run with a group. It felt like we'd only been out a short time before we got to the turnaround where Joan had dropped off water and cups. I could not believe how quickly the time passed and how good it felt.

The best thing was that after, when we got back to the parking lot, Candace pulled out a cooler filled with drinks and a tin of homemade treats. The fast people had added on another few miles so we all finished at the same time and everyone stood around refueling with neon-colored sports drinks and peanut butter cookies.

These runners seemed so different, with different body types and different backgrounds and even different systems of belief—when the conversation turned to politics, Valerie started talking about what races were coming up—but they all seemed devoted to being there each Saturday, and to really care about one another.

Miles and I stayed in the parking lot long after everyone else had left.

We were by far the youngest—some of the runners had kids they had to get home to, or gardens to weed, or work to do. But for me and Miles, 10:30 on a Saturday was still when most of our peers were sleeping in. We walked a few laps around the edge of the parking lot, then sat on the warm asphalt.

"Do you really think Joan is a failure?" I asked. I'd been spending a lot of time thinking about this. If the question surprised Miles, he didn't show it.

"She choked during her last race. She lost confidence."

"Or maybe," I said, "she changed her focus. Maybe she didn't really want what she thought she wanted."

"Why wouldn't you want to go as fast as you can?"

"Well," I said, nibbling on my last bit of cookie, "because

there are other things that matter. You can't be fast forever. No one can. 'Nothing gold can stay,'" I said.

"Can stay what?"

"It's a quote. Google it."

"Huh," Miles said again. He was quiet for a while, and I
thought we'd bumped into a place where we were going to
argue.

"You know," he said finally, "she's probably made more
of an impact with the store than she ever did as a runner.
There are lots of people who used to be fast—and then
didn't do anything significant with running, except complain about how the new crop of runners isn't good enough."

We didn't speak again for a while, just sat on the pave-
ment, leaving big wet spots from our sweat-soaked shorts.

"How's the Tater Tot?" I said. "Haven't seen the little
guy in a while."

"He misses you," Miles said, and then he blushed. "How
about a spud run on Thursday after school? We could go out
to the Kanawha State Forest and do a longish loop on the
trails. Harry says he needs to get out more, that he's in
danger of going from a hot dog to a summer sausage."

"Can't let that happen," I said. "How long is longish?"

"About eleven, but we'll take it easy."

Eleven miles? Today I'd done nine and it felt good.
Could I do two more?

I wasn't sure, but I wanted to go.

So we agreed I'd pick him up at Harry's and drive us to
the forest on Thursday.

24

When weeks went by and I never heard back from the rat lady at the college in Boston, I felt embarrassed. I figured she must have thought I was a dweeb to write her such a long and personal message, if she even bothered to read it.

But when I'd finally stopped cringing every time I remembered it, I got a reply from her.

To: Alice Davis
Subject: Internship?

Dear Alice,

Rodentiaphilia! I love it!

Thank you so much for writing. I've been out of the country (I had to take my students on a trip to Prague!) and am just now catching up on e-mail. I almost missed this wonderful message from you.

Have you figured out what you're going to do next year? It's too bad that your applications didn't work out, but there are so many wonderful colleges and universities in this country, and so many incredible professors to work with, surely you will have a lot of options.

Here's one you might consider: I could offer you a place in my lab for the fall semester. You could do an internship with us and sit in on some courses while you reapply to colleges. I've mentored students who have gone to graduate school all over the country and I'd be happy to put you in touch with them.

This is also a self-interested offer. I rely on students to help me think through experiments and carry them out. Since I'm at a small undergraduate institution instead of a big research university, I don't have a surplus of labor. I do have a student coming in the spring for the second part of her gap year, so having you in the fall would work out well for me. The undergrads are a great group and you would likely enjoy it here.

Think about it and let me know. It would be easy to find you housing and Boston is a great running town.

Best,
Marnie

I had assumed I'd go to one of the two schools that admitted me, neither of which I was crazy about. I knew I only got into Bowdoin because both my parents went there and have given lots of dough to the alumni fund, and I'm pretty sure I got into Trinity because I wrote my supplemental essay about the dad who had the heart attack during our information session. They probably felt like they owed me something.

Mom told me she'd sent a nonrefundable deposit to both schools because while she understood that I might not be ready to make a decision, it was worth losing the money so I would have a choice.

I'd started getting mail from two colleges that each thought I would be in their freshman class next year.

Miles had talked about taking a gap year starting in January when he finished high school but I never thought *I* could do that. I was on a path, the straight-and-narrow course of the college-bound.

Could I step off the hamster wheel I'd been on my whole life?

25

When Potato got in the car, he jumped onto my lap and licked my face like a crazy person.

I couldn't help laughing. He tried to slip his tongue into my mouth, and I said, "No French-kissing today, doodle-bug," and then felt my face turn bright red.

Miles buckled his seat belt and leaned over to grab Potato off me. As he came close, I could smell his shampoo. His shoulder brushed against mine. Potato was wiggling and wagging and it seemed like it took Miles a long time—with his shoulder against mine—to get a grip on the squirming little dude.

He gave me directions to get to the trailhead.

I liked the way he navigated: he gave me plenty of warning and would say, "I'd turn left here," as if I were making a choice and he was just letting me know what he would do if he were in my position. He was the opposite of that bossy Gladys from the GPS.

"Happy brown sign!" Miles said as we passed a sign that read RECREATION AREA 3 MILES and had images of a tent and two hikers with backpacks. "When you see a happy brown sign, you know something good is coming."

I'd never noticed them. I barely remembered what the different colored signs meant from when I had to take my driver's test. I knew yellow stood for caution; brown probably meant recreation. I liked that he'd given it a name and knew that I would always think *happy brown sign* when I saw one.

After we parked and Miles opened the door, Potato charged out of the car and ran around and peed on everything he could find, including:

1. A tire of the only other car in the parking lot.
2. A flower.
3. A lot of trees.
4. The ladder to the slide on the playground across the street.
5. If I hadn't caught him in time, my leg.

Miles slipped a small pack onto his back. I hadn't thought to bring anything to drink. He saw me looking at him and said, "I've got plenty of supplies, including water for the tuber. There should be some out on the trail, but Harry worries if she sees me leave without water for him. I'm a cairn terrier's Sherpa."

He gestured with his head toward the trail and motioned for me to go.

"Wanna?" he said.

I did.

At first it was open and we ran through a grassy meadow. Then the trail slid into the woods. It was single-track, so we had to run in line, not side by side. Potato dashed ahead.

Sometimes he stayed on the trail, sometimes he ventured into the woods to chase squirrels, real or imagined. The trail climbed, and soon I was huffing and shuffling along.

"Do you want to go ahead?" I said to Miles. I wanted to walk, but someone had written on the START wall, *No one ever got better at running hills by walking them.* That went through my mind every time I got to a hill.

Plus, I didn't want Miles to think I was wimping out.

"I'm good," he said. He sure was. He never had to breathe hard. He said, "I like the way you're attacking the hill—slow and steady. You've got natural talent."

It struck me as strange to mention talent in relation to running. It seemed more like something that should apply to culture, like being able to carry a tune, or the way Jenni could look at a piece of material—wood, fabric, discarded Christmas ornaments—and transform it into something else. Running seemed so, well, pedestrian. You put one foot in front of the other to stop yourself from falling. All it took was the decision to keep doing it. You couldn't help but get better.

Miles continued. "Like Remy."

"You saw it!" Hearing he had watched *Ratatouille* felt like a gift.

"I had to do some work to convince Harry. She didn't want to watch a cartoon. Said she stopped watching them with *Fantasia*, which was made by Disney, like, two hundred years ago. But I told her it was important to me, that the movie had been highly recommended by someone I trusted, so she agreed, with a bit of grumbling."

"And?"

"Great thing about Harry. She says she loves being wrong. Now we've been on a binge of watching Pixar films. She said she was mortified to have been so bigoted, to have passed judgment without knowing what she was talking about."

"And what did you think?"

"I think you're awesome."

I was glad he couldn't see my face.

Then he farted. Three times, three little farts in a row.

"Must be ducks around here," he said, and I busted out laughing.

About a minute later, I burped. Really loud.

We both laughed.

Even though the trail was still going up, being so comfortable around him gave me a shot of energy and I felt like I could keep going forever. I also felt kind of brave.

"Look," I said. "There's some stuff I need to tell you."

"That doesn't sound good."

I took a deep breath.

Joan was right. Some conversations are easier when you don't have to face each other. "Well, you may not think I'm awesome anymore. You may think I'm a freak."

"Doubt it."

So I told him about Walter.

He said, "A rat? A real rat?"

"Yes."

He said, "Huh."

So I told him a bunch of funny Walter stories.

He listened and occasionally asked questions that showed it had never occurred to him that rats could be such great companions, but that now he understood. It felt so good to talk about my little dude. I missed him so much.

Then I told Miles how Walter had started to fail and I hadn't noticed. When I had to tell the final part, I couldn't keep running. I slowed to a walk.

After I finished talking, Miles put a hand on my shoulder and I couldn't help it, I began to cry. I didn't want him to know I was crying, so I started running again.

We were quiet for a while and then he said, "So that's why you haven't been around. I thought maybe you just didn't like me."

"No!" I said, too loud as usual.

I didn't turn, but I could hear him chuckle behind me. I was glad we couldn't see each other. I knew we were both smiling.

"There's something else," I said.

"Just so you know, I'm even more convinced of your awesomeness."

"Maybe not when you hear this. Eight of the best colleges in the country think I'm a loser."

I told him about my thwarted plans to go to Yale, and about being rejected from all the other schools. He listened without comment.

Then I told him about the e-mail from the Boston rat lady.

He let out a whoop and said, "If you don't do this, you're nuts."

"Really?"

"Really. It sounds like the perfect thing for you. Who cares about dumb old Yale?"

I thought, I do.

And then I thought, no, I don't.

"I'm pretty sure my parents would be okay with it. They have a bunch of friends in Boston. We've visited there a lot."

"Yeah," he said. He paused, and added in a soft voice, "And then, in the spring, you might want to try WWOOF-ing."

I felt my heart pound, and not from running.

I thought, me? Travel around the world milking rabbits or shoveling bat poop or whatever people did on those farms? I couldn't do that.

We had gotten nearly to the top and the path was starting to flatten out.

Could I? Could I go WWOOFing?

The trail opened into a clearing. You could see all over the valley. It felt like being on the roof of the world.

Miles took off his backpack and plopped down on a big flat rock.

I wasn't ready to sit. I stood tall and noticed how green and full of life the forest was. The air smelled sharp and clean. I could hear birds messing around in the branches of trees and Potato snuffling after them. I held out my arms and twirled and sang as much as I could remember from Cat Stevens's "On the Road to Find Out."

Miles just watched me for a while, with a wide smile on his face. He poured some water into a cup for the spud, then he pulled out a loaf of crusty bread and a jar of something. He held the bread up to his ear and, quoting from *Ratatouille*, said that the crust sounded good. He showed me the jar.

"Nutella. Chocolate and hazelnut. From Harry. She said we should have something sweet today."

He had talked about me to Harry!

I sat next to him and Potato came and lay down alongside my legs, the way Walter used to.

I watched as Miles smoothed a spoonful of the dark brown spread onto a hunk of bread. He handed it to me.

OMG, it was delicious. Nutty and chocolaty—well, enough said.

"You got some on your snoot."

He leaned in close and rubbed the tip of my nose. Even though it now probably had a combo of Nutella, sweat, old makeup, and skin oil on it, he put his finger into his mouth.

I held my breath, watching him, watching the finger.

He moved his hand from his mouth to my cheek.

To the back of my head.

He pulled me close and I could smell his shampoo again, and something else, something a little spicy, a little tart.

He whispered, "You wanna?"

I nodded.

He kissed me.

It was better than I could ever have imagined.

He pulled back, and when I finally opened my eyes, he was looking at me, looking at my face, and into my eyes in a way that made me squirm.

He said, "Woof."

"Woof," I said, and laughed.

Then we said together, "WOOF."

And I kissed him again.

26

It wouldn't be real until I told Jenni.

She was in the kitchen with Mom. I grabbed her skinny arm and was going to drag her to my room, but then I changed my mind.

Instead I sat at the table. Mom got up to go, but I said, "Stay. Please." I told Jenni and Mom in slow-motion what had happened. I lingered over the details. I recounted every single thing Miles had said to me and how I responded. And then I told them about what now seemed like solid plans for next year.

I waited for Mom to comment, to start asking questions about who Miles was and how I'd met him or where I was going to live in Boston, but she didn't. Her hands were clasped around her coffee cup and she watched me as I talked, occasionally nodding and smiling.

Jenni listened the way she always does, as if what I was saying was the secret to the meaning of life. She never interrupted, the way Mom and I often did. Or gave her opinion, the way Mom and I often did. When I was finally finished she said, "Oh Al, I'm so happy for you."

Mom let go of her cup, leaned over, and took both of my

hands in hers. She still hadn't said a word, but her eyes were shiny. She kissed me on the top of my head the way she usually kissed Jenni.

I felt full, and my heart was light in a way it hadn't been for a long time.

27

At graduation, in my *valedictory* ("bidding farewell") speech, I said:

I am a reject.

I was rejected from my first-choice college.

I was rejected from my second-choice college.

And I was rejected from my third-, fourth-, fifth-, sixth-seventh- and eighth-choice colleges.

This seemed like the end of the world.

Then I finally looked up and saw how small I had made my world, how narrow my focus had been. I realized I'd cared about the wrong things and not paid enough attention to the people closest to me. I hadn't taken enough chances.

In the past six months I've spent a lot of time thinking about rejection, failure, and loss. When I look at the people I most admire, many of them have experienced something that looks like failure. But when you take the time to exercise your powers of vision with more imaginative strength, to peer deep into the curves and shifts of how real lives are lived, you see that what happens when you fail is that you get an opportunity to think harder, to think differently.

I used to hate being wrong. If I gave an incorrect answer in class—if I missed the sixth digit of pi or said the Civil War started in 1862—it would burn in me all day. If I got a 98 on a physics test instead of 100 because I left off the units, on the next test I would check every answer for units until my eyeballs bled. I stand before you now as valedictorian, top of the class, not because I cared so much about learning, but because I was afraid of not getting things right.

Along the way, I missed out on a lot.

I didn't spend enough time listening to the people I love, or getting to know my fellow students, or being involved in the community, or even hanging out at games where people throw projectiles at one another's heads. Though that last one may have been the result of an evolutionarily useful self-protective instinct.

My unwillingness to participate was partly out of a fear of being rebuffed and also a reaction against expectations. I know that many of the students who applied to the schools I was rejected by do just the opposite: they are involved in everything, spend all their time being busy, shuttling between clubs and practices and contests and conferences and they never have a moment to really think.

As it turns out, most of them got rejected too.

It's easy to be a critic. We know from President Theodore Roosevelt that it's not the critic who counts, not the man who carps and quibbles, not the woman who says "I shoulda" or "I woulda," but the person who says, strong and loud and unafraid, "I tried."

The way to change the world—and since this is a

graduation speech, I feel it's my responsibility to tell you, with all the conviction that a teenager who's never done anything in her life can muster, the way to change the world—is for each of us to learn to embrace being wrong.

I want to be able to make mistakes and then admit them. To apologize if necessary, and then to recalibrate, to rethink, to reconsider, to look again, to look more closely, and to see where I went astray. I want to be able to say that I love making mistakes.

I'm not there yet, so please know that if anyone points out any errors in this speech, I may first argue and then I'll go to my room and cry.

But I want to develop into the kind of person who can say, without shame and with real delight, "I was wrong." Because once I know I'm wrong, I can go about getting to the point where I am right. We recognize mistakes only in retrospect. Being afraid to make mistakes is more growth-stunting than smoking cigarettes. Self-satisfaction is the road to mediocrity.

Six months ago, after being rejected from the only school I ever wanted to go to, I started running. At first I hated it.

Then I liked it.

And then it weirdly turned into a part of who I am.

I once asked a friend, a good friend, who is a runner, a very good runner, to tell me what I was doing wrong. I wanted to get better. He said something that has stuck with me. He said, "Running is the act of catching yourself before you fall."

Even so, I realized it's not the worst thing to fall.

I want to throw myself into the world and at new things. That means I will fail at some and succeed at others.

I will fall, I will fail, I will move on.

I want to know great devotions and great enthusiasms.

I have already experienced great love. I was in love with someone who weighed less than a pint of milk and who couldn't be bothered to keep his own tail clean. Regardless of species or tail hygiene, I loved my rat, Walter. And when he died, I learned—I'm learning—that I will survive the loss, even if it means the world will never look the same again.

I may be a reject. But I am not a failure. At least, not as long as I keep trying.

28

I couldn't believe it when, after I finished speaking, the entire audience stood and cheered.

We marched across the stage and the principal flipped our tassels and handed us our degrees and we tossed our hats to the sky. There was a giant roar when Jenni's name was called. She had blinged out her mortarboard, making it cool and elegant and funky and fun all at once. Her dad was there. He hadn't had a drink in a couple of weeks and Jenni was feeling optimistic, like maybe this time he'd be able to stay sober. My mom had asked him to sit with our family. Miles was sitting with them too. Mom had invited everyone over to our house for a catered brunch afterward.

I walked toward them. Walter-the-Man stood thisclose to a woman with chin-length brown hair. She wore a trim suit that managed to look both stylish and comfortable. Tim Gunn would have approved.

Walter-the-Man grabbed me around the shoulders and said, "Good job, sport."

"Don't call me sport, chief."

"I want you to meet someone. This is Deborah."

OMG. The woman I knew more about than anyone I had never met before. Had they gotten back together? Walter-the-Man winked at me.

Deborah's eyes were rimmed with red and she was holding a tissue.

"That was wonderful," she said. "I feel like I know you, Alice. Walt talks about you all the time. That speech— I've heard a lot of graduation speeches—you made me laugh, and you made me cry. You nailed it."

"Thanks," I said.

"But you got something wrong."

"I did?" Oh crap.

"Yes," she said, nodding and smiling. "You weren't rejected."

"No, I got that right. I was rejected. I can show you the letters."

"No," she said, still nodding yes. "You weren't rejected. Your applications were denied. If you failed, it was in not showing on paper how extraordinary you are. Your applications were rejected, not you."

I could see why Walter-the-Man liked Deborah and I hoped that they were back together.

Joan—I hadn't even known she was there—gave me one of her tight Joan-hugs. You couldn't believe such a tiny person could squeeze so hard.

Everyone huddled around and Joan handed me a bag, a light backpack with a cinched-tight drawstring, like the kind Miles often used.

"Open it," Joan said.

I did. I dug my hand in and pulled out a race bib.

"Half marathon. Tomorrow. You're driving up with Miles, Nikki, and Owen."

"I can't do a half marathon," I said.

And then I asked, "Can I?"

"Of course you can," Joan said.

She was right. I could do a half marathon.

"Keep looking in the bag," Jenni said.

"You guys have met?" I said.

Joan threw an arm around Jenni and said, "We've all conspired on this. Walt insisted on bankrolling your entry fee. And he's taking you guys out for a steak dinner after the race."

"I figured it would be cheaper than a meth lab," Walter-the-Man said, and Deborah shook her head.

"Keep looking," Jenni said, bouncing on her toes. I fished out a box I recognized right away. I'd fondled these in the store. It was a Garmin wristwatch GPS.

Dad said, "It doesn't talk, I'm sure you're happy to know. Now you'll have lots of data about your pace, your distance, your calories burned. It may even make you a cup of coffee and clean your room."

"There's more," Jenni said, flapping her arms. Jenni sometimes flapped when she got excited.

I reached in and found what I thought was a stick of Body Glide, but it turned out to be deodorant.

"That's from me," said Walter-the-Man. "I don't want to be around a stinker." Deborah elbowed him in the ribs.

There was a pair of socks and a hat and a water bottle, all of which said *Runner's Edge*. Joan smiled.

And something else, a pair of arm warmers, black with red flames on them.

"Those are from me," Miles said. "Because you're like fire—you burn hot and fast," and I got all embarrassed, especially when there was a giant "Aaawwww" from the group.

Then I pulled out a singlet and held it against me. It was the perfect size and in purple, my favorite color.

"Look at the back," Jenni said, now more quiet and subdued.

Printed in careful letters it said, *Running in memory of Walter*. There was a small silhouette of a rat.

I was about to start crying when Jenni said, "One more."

At the bottom of the bag I found a small box. A where's-the-box kind of box.

I opened it.

Inside was a tiny figure of a runner on a gold chain.

I turned to Mom and wrapped my arms around her, breathing in her perfume. I didn't realize until that moment that was what home smelled like.

She held me close and whispered, "I'm so proud of you, Al."

And I whispered back, "I love you, Mommy. I love you so much."

And she said, "I love you more."

And then I said really loud, "NO, I LOVE YOU MORE," and we laughed and kept hugging.

And she said, "Fine."

And I said, "Fine."

And then Walter-the-Man bellowed, "ENOUGH. TIME FOR BRUNCH!"

29

The sun is shining, shining with all his might. Nikki is driving fast, and she and Owen are arguing about everything from genetically modified food to whether *all right* should be one word or two, while Miles and I, still morning-sleepy in the backseat, *furtively* ("characterized by stealth") hold hands.

I am nervous about the race, but I know I can do it.

When we get to the start, the three of them take off to warm up and I look around and see a bunch of people I know from working at the store. David is doing stretches next to a tree, and Jeff is busy putting Body Glide in places you probably shouldn't be touching in public. Candace has her hair in pigtails, looking cuter than a middle-aged woman has a right to, and Valerie is helping another woman pin on her number. I've seen more than a few men check out Ruth's tanned, movie-star-beautiful legs.

These are my peeps. I have become a runner.

I glance down at the race bib pinned carefully onto my purple singlet and can already see it hanging on the START wall at the store. When the race is over, I will write on it, *Alice, daring greatly.*

During the race, I will think about how hard I've had to work to make it to this place and how happy I am to have arrived. I can't believe it's only been six months since that first wet, miserable eight-minute slog on New Year's Day.

We gather at the start. We're all crammed together and I smell sunscreen, spilled energy drinks, and body odor. People are wearing shorts and skirts and singlets and T-shirts from other races. At the front of the pack, a bunch of skinny guys without shirts are striding out to warm up. I can't see Miles, but I know he's there.

After it's over, I will listen to him talk about how the race went for him, and Nikki and Owen will each narrate their own adventures.

And then I'll tell the story of how it was for me.

We are all here, we are all in the arena.

The gun goes off and I begin to run.

NOTE TO READERS

When I worked in college admissions at Duke University, one of my student friends said, "Rachel, you're the reason I don't run."

She explained that since I didn't start until age thirty, she figured she still had years to go before she laced up her running shoes.

I've now run something like fifty or sixty marathons and ultramarathons—50Ks, 50-milers, a crazy 100-mile stage race in the Himalayas. I've led pace groups at marathons, coached a season of high school cross-country, and made great friends on weekly Sunday morning long runs. Running has gotten me trips to India, Thailand, Singapore, and Israel and has been my preferred way to celebrate good things, to think through hard decisions, and to get the ya-yas out when I'm mad.

Senior year of high school, I was often mad. I worried that if I didn't get into my first-choice college, life would be over. If I had been able to go for a run, maybe I wouldn't have continually locked my keys in my car and snarled at my mother for the months I waited for fat and thin envelopes.

The truth is I didn't know jack about any of the colleges I'd applied to. The summer after my junior year, I went to France to restore a historic château (translation: I lugged around loads of dusty rocks) with a bunch of French and American high school and college students. The high school kids nattered incessantly about their applications. The two Yalies there, Win and Duffy, were the most intimidating, intelligent, scary people I'd ever met. I wanted to be just like them.

All through high school I wrote. I wrote poetry, some really bad, and some a little less bad. I won contests. I got into Yale, I had always believed, because I'd written a good essay. Later, when I worked in admissions, I learned that the "dead grandma essay" is a kind of cliché and that the personal statement doesn't matter all that much in terms of the outcome.

At Yale, I felt small and stupid and like someone had made a mistake by admitting me. I was thirty-five years old by the time I paid off my student loans and I hadn't written for pleasure since high school.

After graduation, I worked in publishing. And then I quit and slid down the ladder of social mobility. I ran a lot, rode horses, and ate popcorn for dinner. When I was tired and hungry, I got a job working in admissions at Duke. Three years later I left feeling dirty, implicated in the process by which I traveled around the country getting kids all excited about applying so that we could reject them in April. I saw myself as a prophet of false hope.

In my book *Admissions Confidential* (I've always hated that title; I wanted to call it *Admission Impossible*), I tried to lay bare the way things worked so that kids, and their parents, would know the real poop. Even if you do everything "right," you're still probably not going to get in. And this is what I've come to believe: Where you go to college matters not at all, and also a great deal, but not in the ways most people think. You can get a great education anywhere and can snag a fantastic job without a fancy degree. What counts is what you do in college and the people you meet there; your identity gets formed in ways that will last, affected by the company you keep. The dining hall can be a more important place of learning than the classroom.

After I left my job in admissions, dead broke, my BFF hectored me into doing college counseling for her son. I realized that a thoughtful approach to the admissions process could make it a real and meaningful journey of self-discovery, a cool thing to witness. I've learned so much from the high school students I've worked with (a number of whom read an early draft of this book) and had a lot of fun doing it. I'm not an admissions counselor anymore. I've got a day job as a college professor, though I still sometimes eat popcorn for dinner.

But here, for what it's worth, is my best advice about the college admissions process:

- Anyone who takes your money and says they can get you into college is either a liar or a fool. Probably a liar. A greedy liar.
- Figure out what you're passionate about—Japanese anime, reading poetry, finding alternative energy sources for developing countries—and figure out a way to pursue that. Doing "everything" will just make you tired.
- Practice SATing. You don't need an expensive course, but it's a coachable test. As with running, the more you practice, the better you'll get.
- Write letters to the teachers you're asking for recommendations. Remind them of the work you've done in class and mention ideas and concepts that particularly intrigued you. This will help them write good—not just positive—recommendations.
- Follow directions and send in what's required. If you pad your application, readers will wonder what you're trying to compensate for. In the file room at Duke they used to say, "The thicker the file, the thicker the kid."
- Get applications done the summer before senior year.

The short essays are the hardest to write because they all end up sounding the same. Be specific. Be vivid.
- Make sure you have eight (8!) first-choice schools, at varying levels of selectivity, any of which you would be thrilled to attend.
- Don't let money determine where you apply. It might affect where you go, but there's a lot of financial aid available. Check out www.finaid.org.
- Write your essay in the form of an e-mail to a friendly relative you rarely see. Show it to people who know you and love you enough to be critical. Listen if they say it's boring or doesn't sound like you. Better to admit to your flaws than to brag about your accomplishments.
- Consider taking a gap year. Most colleges will let you defer after you've been admitted.
- Know that wherever you end up—even if it's your safety school—will likely turn out to be the right place for you.

When my friends from high school and college find out that I'm a writer they're not surprised. But they yowl with laughter when they learn about my running. *You?* They say. *You're* a runner?

Yep. The person who invented injuries to get out of gym class runs ultramarathons. How did I get from there to here? Easy. I just put one foot in front of the other and ran.

But for those who want some more specific tips:

- Get fitted for shoes at a running store. (If you have boobs, buy a running bra.) You don't need any other equipment at first. You *can* run in jeggings.
- Start slower than you think you can go. Way slower. Run so slowly you feel like you could hold that pace all day.
- If you need to walk, walk.
- Build up your distance gradually.
- Expect to have bad days. Everyone has bad days. Sometimes a lot in a row. Don't get discouraged, just keeping lacing up your shoes.
- You won't need water unless you'll be out for a long time— or it's very hot.
- Just get your butt out the door. Say you'll only go for ten minutes. Or one mile. Or around the block. Once you're out there, you can change your mind. (Once you're out there, you will likely change your mind.)
- Always run facing traffic. And on the softest possible

surface. Asphalt is better than concrete, and dirt is best of all.

- Listen to a good book. I once accidentally ran for five hours because I couldn't stop listening to Donna Tartt's *The Secret History*. If you wear earphones, make sure you can still hear traffic.
- If you're a program-follower, follow a program.
- If you're a log-keeper, keep a log.
- Be yourself. We run, like we make sandwiches, in our own image. Think about who you are and what motivates you. Do you need a goal? Sign up for a 5K. Are you a social person? Ask a friend to join you. Do you like instruction? Find a club.

It delights me to hear from people who are just starting to run and from those who have set or achieved goals. I love knowing if anything I've ever said has helped anyone even a little bit. I can't promise wisdom or even wit, but I will respond as quickly and as honestly as I can. Find me at www.racheltoor.com. Friend me on Facebook. Tell me your story.

ACKNOWLEDGMENTS

As every author knows and most acknowledge, writing a book is hard and lonely work, but if you're fortunate, you get help from good and generous people along the way. I'm grateful for the smart early readings I got from Julie Bramlet, Robin Ebenstein, Malini Gandhi, Candace Karu, Natalie Kusz, Jane Ligon, Ruth Monnig, Rachel Scott, and Hannah Voves. I heart my agent, Elise Capron, and am indebted to everyone at the sunny Sandra Dijkstra Literary Agency. My experience at Farrar Straus Giroux Books for Young Readers has been the stuff of author fantasy. Editorial assistant Angie Chen started running after she read the proposal. Some of her thoughts, sentences, and aches are—shockingly—exactly the same as Alice's, especially the funny stuff. I'm grateful to my rocking publicity and marketing team at Macmillan, MacRunners Ellen Cormier, Molly Brouillette, Kelly McCauley, and (not-yet-a-runner) Kathryn Little. Getting early feedback from the veteran editorial staff at FSG was—how do I put this?—freaking amazing. I must confess to a huge girl crush on editorial director Joy Peskin. About executive editor Wes Adams, I have nothing to say. (Beyond what is written in the dedication to this book. It makes him twitchy when I gush.)